HERCULE POIROT
AND THE
GREENSHORE FOLLY

ALSO BY AGATHA CHRISTIE

Mystery

The Man in the Brown Suit
The Secret of Chimneys
The Seven Dials Mystery
The Mysterious Mr. Quin
The Sittaford Mystery
The Hound of Death
The Listerdale Mystery
Why Didn't They Ask Evans?
Parker Pyne Investigates
Murder Is Easy
And Then There Were None
Towards Zero
Death Comes as the End
Sparkling Cyanide
Crooked House
They Came to Baghdad
Destination Unknown
Spider's Web*
The Unexpected Guest*
Ordeal by Innocence
The Pale Horse
Endless Night
Passenger To Frankfurt
Problem at Pollensa Bay
While the Light Lasts

Poirot

The Mysterious Affair at Styles
The Murder on the Links
Poirot Investigates
The Murder of Roger Ackroyd
The Big Four
The Mystery of the Blue Train
Black Coffee*
Peril at End House
Lord Edgware Dies

Murder on the Orient Express
Three-Act Tragedy
Death in the Clouds
The ABC Murders
Murder in Mesopotamia
Cards on the Table
Murder in the Mews
Dumb Witness
Death on the Nile
Appointment With Death
Hercule Poirot's Christmas
Sad Cypress
One, Two, Buckle My Shoe
Evil Under the Sun
Five Little Pigs
The Hollow
The Labours of Hercules
Taken at the Flood
Mrs. McGinty's Dead
After the Funeral
Hickory Dickory Dock
Dead Man's Folly
Cat Among the Pigeons
The Adventure of the Christmas Pudding
The Clocks
Third Girl
Hallowe'en Party
Elephants Can Remember
Poirot's Early Cases
Curtain: Poirot's Last Case

Marple

The Murder at the Vicarage
The Thirteen Problems
The Body in the Library
The Moving Finger
A Murder is Announced

They Do It With Mirrors
A Pocket Full of Rye
4.50 from Paddington
The Mirror Crack'd from Side to Side
A Caribbean Mystery
At Bertram's Hotel
Nemesis
Sleeping Murder
Miss Marple's Final Cases

Tommy & Tuppence

The Secret Adversary
Partners in Crime
N or M?
By the Pricking of My Thumbs
Postern of Fate

Published as Mary Westmacott

Giant's Bread
Unfinished Portrait
Absent in the Spring
The Rose and the Yew Tree
A Daughter's a Daughter
The Burden

Memoirs

An Autobiography
Come, Tell Me How You Live
The Grand Tour

Plays and Stories

Akhnaton
The Mousetrap and Other Plays
The Floating Admiral (contributor)
Star Over Bethlehem

* novelised by Charles Osborne

Agatha Christie

HERCULE POIROT
AND THE
GREENSHORE FOLLY

HarperCollins*Publishers*

HarperCollins*Publishers*
1 London Bridge Street,
London SE1 9GF
www.harpercollins.co.uk

HarperCollins*Publishers*
Macken House, 39/40 Mayor Street Upper
Dublin 1, D01 C9W8, Ireland

First published 2014
10

ISBN 978-0-00-754639-8

Typeset in Fournier MT

Printed and bound in the UK using 100%
renewable electricity at CPI Group (UK) Ltd

CONTENTS

Introduction by Tom Adams
7

Preface by Mathew Prichard
19

HERCULE POIROT AND
THE GREENSHORE FOLLY
25

'Agatha Christie and The Greenshore Folly'
by John Curran
147

Introduction
by Tom Adams

MORE THAN half a century ago – 1962 to be precise – my impressively-named and enthusiastic agent, Virgil Pomfret, took me to meet the art director of Fontana Paperbacks, Patsy Cohen. On her desk was a copy of *The Collector*, John Fowles' first published novel. It had been commissioned by Tony Colwell, art director at Jonathan Cape, and was my first serious attempt at *trompe l'oeil* painting for jacket art. It was a good time to be producing art for book covers. Good art was notably lacking in this field, particularly for paperbacks. In fact, the general standard was pretty dire, and the time was ripe for raising the bar. Up to then I had enjoyed doing serious paintings for hardback jackets, which included John Fowles' *The Magus*, Patrick White's *Vivisector* and David Storey's *Saville*. Paperback covers were more often than not the poor second class products of publishers' lists (with exceptions such as the original typographical Penguin covers), but virtually no serious attempt had been made to commission good art for paperbacks. However with the enthusiastic encouragement of Mark Collins, Virgil Pomfret and Patsy Cohen, I think we succeeded in doing just that.

From 1962 onwards, my relationship with Agatha Christie developed and prospered as I produced more than a hundred cover paintings for her books over twenty-five years. To begin with I simply enjoyed doing a good job. There were inevitably some failures and I know that I didn't always please Agatha or her family. I am frequently asked if I met Agatha. I'm afraid the answer is no. Arrangements *were* made for various meetings; I did meet Rosalind Hicks, her daughter, Edmund Cork, her agent, and other members of her entourage, but Agatha's legendary reticence and occasional illness prevented her from accepting invitations for us to meet. In retrospect I think it was just as well; it might have been embarrassing for both of us to discuss the likes and dislikes of various cover images. Nevertheless, for me it is a niggling regret. More recently, since my exhibition of Agatha Christie cover paintings at Torquay Museum in 2012, I have on several occasions met Mathew Prichard, a devoted and eloquent advocate of his grandmother's achievements. Mathew and his wife Lucy have been a tower of strength and gratifyingly appreciative of my work. They helped and encouraged me in my recent endeavours on Agatha's behalf, in particular while working on the cover painting for *Hercule Poirot and the Greenshore Folly*, and they arranged with the National Trust to make Greenway House and garden available for my research. Once, after a delightful lunch with Mathew and Lucy at Ferry Cottage, and with my wife, the children's writer Georgie Adams, we were taken on a memorable boat trip on the River Dart.

I was delighted when David Brawn, Publisher of Agatha Christie at HarperCollins, asked me to do this special cover painting for a so-far unpublished story. It is a shorter version of the excellent *Dead Man's Folly* and a great excuse for me to revisit Greenway. Agatha's second husband Max Mallowan described Greenway as 'this little paradise', and it was for Agatha 'the loveliest place in the world'. And it is. The handsome, foursquare, no-nonsense Georgian house is in many ways an embodiment of its famous literary owner. But it is the garden that is the true paradise. In my painting I have tried, within the constrictions of being true to the story, to embody its extraordinary beauty and magic. It is without doubt one of the iconic places of the West Country – that West Country with its rain-soaked and occasionally sun-soaked landscape, haunted moors and secret bosky woodlands, fringed by sea and rocky shores.

Greenway has a flamboyant garden, almost tropical in places and bordered by the Dart, and is now owned by the National Trust. For Agatha it provided a safe retreat from an often intrusive outside world, a world she was fascinated by and acutely observed, but into which she had no wish to be integrated.

This great detective story writer, this skilled puzzle and plot maker, was the inspiration for my work on her books. My painting for this story is a tribute to her house and garden but, nevertheless, it had to fulfil its function as an illustration. I know that Agatha instinctively disliked visual depictions of actual incidents, scenes and human figures, and in particular insisted that Hercule Poirot and Miss Marple must not be shown on the covers. Though

Collins tended to adhere to these rules, her American publishers *demanded* more literal imagery, as demonstrated by the US version of *Dead Man's Folly*, reproduced on the endpapers of this book. I have largely obeyed this sensible injunction but it is right to break rules sometimes as I have for the cover of *The Greenshore Folly*, in which there is some pure illustration, for instance: the house, the boathouse, the ferry bell and Battery; the magnolia (one of Agatha's favourite flowers), the face of Lady Stubbs, the fallen oak and folly; even a slightly fantasised portrait of Agatha herself in a cherished garden nook. And there is a suggestion of a convivial crowd on the front lawn. All this is woven into what I hope is a pictorial tribute to Greenway.

Readers may note that I thatched the boathouse, as described in the story. Today it has a slate roof, but Mathew Prichard remembers that *was* originally thatched. So I have unwittingly restored the building to its former glory!

I make no claims to be a great artist in the same league as Francis Bacon, Lucian Freud or Graham Sutherland. Nevertheless I consider myself to be a good painter and illustrator and worthy I hope of a place somewhere in the middle of the pantheon of British 20th/21st-century art. Incidentally Graham Sutherland became a friend and mentor in the mid-fifties when I was a close neighbour in the Kentish village of Trottiscliffe. My visits to his White House studio and his to my Oast House studio were highlights of my early life as an artist. That I have been lucky enough to have survived into the 21st century and *still* working in my eighties is largely due to the care and loving support of my family and dear friends, not to mention great and understanding publishers and patrons, including Jonathan Cape and HarperCollins. John Fowles generously placed me in 'one of the pleasantest traditions in English art, which goes back essentially to the great woodcut school of the 1860s; and descends through Rackham, Dulac, the Detmold brothers to our own day. Tom stands honourably in that long line . . .' This is all very fine but it is the stimulation of great writers like John Fowles and Agatha Christie that inspired me in my career as an illustrator and cover artist. And I have the temerity to compare myself as an artist to Agatha as a crime novelist. Patient research and dedicated craftsmanship are key to our success. I have always thought that an infinite capacity to take pains was a somewhat inadequate definition of genius, but it is a good part of that elusive quality. Undeniably Christie had that quality, that magic ingredient. Whether or not I do is for others to decide.

Over the years I have had a growing conviction that Agatha Christie was without doubt pre-eminent as a writer of crime fiction. She was a weaver of spells, someone who leads us up and down the garden path, round and round in circles, only to deposit us in an unexpected place. *Oh good heavens*, we say. *We didn't see that coming!* From the first words of advice she received from her friend, Eden Philpotts, Agatha learned that writing was a craft as well as an art and that there are methods and tricks for overcoming stylistic and technical obstacles.

Agatha's work is a gift to the visual artist. Characters, locations, and objects provide a rich choice of subjects, but the lack of specific detail in her descriptions allow the illustrator to imagine and manipulate. As for imagination, Agatha had it in spades. According to Janet Morgan in *Agatha Christie – A Biography*, she was deeply affected by two books: J.W. Dunne's

Experiment With Time and *The Mysterious Universe* by Sir James Jeans, inspiring her to write to Max in 1930:

> 'I understand very little of it but it fills me with nebulous ideas. How queer it would be if *God* were in the future – something we never created or imagined but who is not yet – supposing him to be not *Cause* but *Effect* . . . It's fun to play with ideas – that God has made the world as it is and is pleased with it seems certainly not so. Originally man starved to death and froze to death (on top of coal in the ground) and every plague and pestilence caused by Man's stupidity was put down to "God's Will". If life on this planet is an accident, quite unforeseen, and against all the principles of the solar system – how amazingly interesting – and when may it end? In some complete and marvellous Consciousness . . .'

Janet Morgan's excellent biography discusses how Agatha was a prolific and ingenious fantasist. She 'dreamt vividly, remembered and talked of her dreams, relished them – dreams of flying . . .' I have the same propensity to fantasise and dream, especially dreams of flying, and I've always thought this is one of the many reasons I empathise so well with Agatha in her books.

However, Agatha was also a very down-to-earth person. Her own autobiography shows something of her humanity and wit:

'I don't like crowds, being jammed up against people, loud voices, noise, protracted talking, parties, and especially cocktail parties, cigarette smoke and smoking generally, any kind of drink except in cooking, marmalade, oysters, lukewarm food, grey skies, the feet of birds, or indeed the feel of a bird altogether. Final and fiercest dislike: the taste and smell of hot milk.

'I like sunshine, apples, almost any kind of music, railway trains, numerical puzzles and anything to do with numbers, going to the sea, bathing and swimming, silence, sleeping, dreaming, eating, the smell of coffee, lilies of the valley, most dogs, and going to the theatre.

'I could make much better lists, much grander-sounding, much more *important*, but there again it wouldn't be me, and I suppose I must resign myself to *being* me.'

Agatha worked by herself: 'The most blessed thing about being an author is that you do it in private and in your own time'. I profoundly echo these sentiments! My working conditions are a studio stacked with stuff, books everywhere and everything extremely untidy. I get the feeling that on the much smaller scale of a writer's workspace Agatha was not that much more concerned with order and tidiness than I am. When asked on BBC's radio programme, *Close-Up*, about her process of working, Agatha admitted: 'The disappointing truth is that I haven't much method'. And in John Curran's comprehensively perceptive book, *Agatha Christie's Murder in the Making*, he points out: 'She thrived mentally on chaos, it stimulated her more than neat order; rigidity stifled her creative process.' This was her method and it works for me too. Out of *my* chaos, sketches and multiple reference notes, my finished painting emerges.

Archaeology is something else Agatha and I have in common. She was married to archaeologist Sir Max

Mallowan. My eldest son, Professor Jonathan Adams, is a marine archaeologist. He was Deputy Director of the excavation and raising of the *Mary Rose* and assembles and recreates a logical whole from an unlikely jumble of apparently unrelated bits and pieces – much as I do as an artist – and he is a fine painter. In our own ways we both share much in common with Agatha's method of writing, and I think the processes and activities involved in archaeology are similar to the writing of detective stories: the assembly of pieces, finding facts, following clues, digging below the surface, and taking leaps of imagination. . .

As well as writing books, Agatha Christie was also a very accomplished playwright. My own passion for the theatre began with memories of my parents' active life producing and acting in amateur dramatics. I was privileged to meet many of their theatrical friends such as Flora Robson and Sybil Thorndike, and I have many happy memories of being taken to theatres in London and Paris. My mother, Constance, was a pupil of Dame Carrie Tubbs at the Guildhall School of Music, though regrettably she gave up singing when she got married. Agatha trained as a singer, but she gave it up for writing.

With the painting of the new cover for *Hercule Poirot and the Greenshore Folly*, my association with Agatha Christie as her cover artist now exceeds fifty years. I hope that I will have the opportunity to do more. My conviction about this remarkable author that has steadily grown over the many years of our association can be summed up no better than this quote from a *News Chronicle* reviewer which appears in John Curran's *Agatha Christie's Murder in the Making*: 'Mrs Christie is the greatest genius at inventing detective plots that has ever lived or will ever live'. I couldn't put it better myself.

Tom Adams
Cornwall
January 2014

Preface

by Mathew Prichard

UNUSUALLY FOR Agatha Christie, *Dead Man's Folly* – the book which evolved out of this novella – was written around a specific location, in this case Greenway House on the River Dart in South Devon. Greenway was where Nima (which is what I called my grandmother) used to spend her summer holidays almost from the time she bought it in 1938 until she died in 1976. It is now 15 years since Greenway was acquired by the National Trust and subsequently opened to the public.

Last year ITV's series *Agatha Christie's Poirot* starring David Suchet shot its final film there, *Dead Man's Folly*, and so a series that had begun in 1989 with *The Adventure of the Clapham Cook* ended in a blaze of glory at Greenway itself. Neither Nima, nor my late mother Rosalind, who had a lot to do with setting up the TV series in the beginning, could have wished for anything better. It was as if Hercule Poirot had come home.

As luck would have it, we were blessed with wonderful summer weather, and the last day of shooting in front of the house – a scene that was not in itself dramatically very significant – was none the less poignant as it featured David Suchet, in full Poirot regalia, mincing up Greenway's front steps in his own inimitable way and knocking on the door. Eventually, after three repeats of the same action, we heard the time-honoured words – 'it's a wrap' – and there was not a dry eye in the house, or rather on the lawn, where a large crowd had come to celebrate the ending of one of the world's best loved TV series, and the portrayal of one of our best loved literary characters, Hercule Poirot, by one of our best loved character actors, David Suchet. If anyone had told Nima (who sadly never met David Suchet) that a series of this magnitude and popularity would be made continuously over a period of 25 years, I am sure that she would not have believed it.

My particular affection for *Dead Man's Folly* extends back to long before the filming of the TV series, though. The book was published in 1956, when I was 13, coinciding with both the time I was beginning to enjoy reading Nima's books, and when as a schoolboy I spent my summer holidays at Greenway with my family including, of course, Nima. I cannot say that I ever remember a fête on the lawn, but I certainly remember smaller events there, as Greenway was host to an ever-growing selection of literary and theatrical friends (this was the heyday of Nima's career as a West End playwright), with plenty of friends of my step-grandfather Max Mallowan from the world of archaeology added for good measure. Nima never based her characters entirely on real-life people, but I would be lying if I did not admit to recognising snippets of Sir George and Lady Stubbs, and particularly Mrs Folliatt, from actual people whom she knew. Nor was I surprised when I found out that *Dead Man's Folly* featured hitch-hikers. We were familiar with the occasional hitch-hiker from the nearby youth hostel called Maypool.

But I suppose *Dead Man's Folly* evokes two particular memories from my childhood that I find particularly poignant: one a person, one a place. The person is Ariadne Oliver, who, although rather more boisterous than Nima would ever be, did have something of her enthusiasm, her love of apples, and a writer's curiosity that reminds me very much of Nima herself. She appeared in seven novels, six of them with Poirot, and Zoë Wanamaker gives an excellent performance in the film. The place is the boathouse, where the poor victim is found murdered. Nima and I used to walk down to Greenway's boathouse in the afternoon, watch the pleasure cruisers sail by (the *Kiloran*, *Pride of Paignton*, *Brixham Belle* and those wonderful paddle streamers, one of which I am delighted to say is still in working order). The tour guides on these boats would always refer to Greenway, usually inaccurately, as the home of Agatha Christie (rather than, strictly speaking, her holiday home), and though we could hear their voices as they sailed past, never do I remember them actually recognising her as she sat inconspicuously in the boathouse with her grandson!

As I read the book again now, I do seem to remember reading it originally on publication as a young teenager and understanding perhaps for the first time a little more about the construction of a detective story in relation to real people and real places, because I was familiar with those in this particular book. This authenticity is of course one of the reasons why Nima's books still seem so real and convincing today. Back then, the books based around archaeology and the Middle East were pure fiction to me, although Nima used exactly the same techniques, drawing on characteristics of real people and factual landmarks and adding a fictional dimension, just as she did with *Dead Man's Folly*. I hope one day that I will be able to visit Nimrud, the Pyramids in Egypt, or some other locations which inspired Nima, so that I can see them as she did. I recently visited one specific place of inspiration in Tenerife in the Canary Islands, the setting for a Harley Quin story called 'The Man from the Sea' (in the book *The Mysterious Mr Quin*) – it is a brilliant short story, and all the better for having been there.

As you probably know, my family gave Greenway to the National Trust in 1999 and it is open to the public for most of the year. Everyone can now visit the boathouse where the murder took place, or relax on a chair near where Hattie Stubbs sat and be polite to the hikers who are now allowed to enter the grounds. You may also find that the National Trust shop has the finest collection of Agatha Christie books in the West of England. Though *Dead Man's Folly* is unusual in being so closely based on a real place, it is not the only Agatha Christie book that has echoes of Greenway. If you enjoy it, you should certainly read *Five Little Pigs* as well, with a murder on Greenway's Battery!

Finally, one of the words I have often chosen to describe Agatha Christie's books and films is 'welcoming', and I do think that Robyn Brown and Gary Calland, the two General Managers the Trust has employed since 1999, and all their staff, have surpassed themselves in making Greenway as welcoming a place as Nima did when I was young. I hope that having read this book, and maybe watched the film with David Suchet, that you can visit the original location. What a treat you have in store!

Mathew Prichard
Monmouth
January 2014

HERCULE POIROT
AND THE
GREENSHORE FOLLY

CHAPTER ONE

IT WAS Miss Lemon, Poirot's efficient secretary, who took the telephone call.

Laying aside her shorthand notebook, she raised the receiver and said without emphasis, 'Trafalgar 8137.'

Hercule Poirot leaned back in his upright chair and closed his eyes. His fingers beat a meditative soft tattoo on the edge of the table. In his head he continued to compose the polished period of the letter he had been dictating.

Placing her hand over the receiver, Miss Lemon asked in a low voice, 'Will you accept a personal call from Lapton, Devon?'

Poirot frowned. The place meant nothing to him.

'The name of the caller?' he demanded cautiously.

Miss Lemon spoke into the mouthpiece.

'*Air-raid?*' she asked doubtingly. 'Oh, yes – what was the last name again?'

Once more she turned to Hercule Poirot.

'Mrs. Ariadne Oliver.'

Hercule Poirot's eyebrows shot up. A memory rose up in his mind: windswept grey hair . . . an eagle profile . . .

He rose and replaced Miss Lemon at the telephone.

'Hercule Poirot speaks,' he announced grandiloquently.

'Is that Mr. Hercules Porrot speaking personally?' the suspicious voice of the telephone operator demanded.

Poirot assured her that that was the case.

'You're through to Mr. Porrot,' said the voice.

Its thin reedy accents were replaced by a magnificent booming contralto which caused Poirot hastily to shift the receiver a couple of inches further from his ear.

'Mr. Poirot, is that really *you?*' demanded Mrs. Oliver.

'Myself in person, Madame.'

'This is Mrs. Oliver. I don't know if you'll remember me –'

'But of course I remember you, Madame. Who could forget you?'

'Well, people do sometimes,' said Mrs. Oliver. 'Quite often, in fact. I don't think that I've got a very distinctive personality. Or perhaps it's because I'm always doing different things to my hair. But all that's neither here nor there. I hope I'm not interrupting you when you're frightfully busy?'

'No, no, you do not derange me in the least.'

'Good gracious – I'm sure I don't want to drive you out of your mind. The fact is, I *need* you.'

'Need me?'

'Yes, at once. Can you take an aeroplane?'

'I do not take aeroplanes. They make me sick.'

'They do me, too. Anyway, I don't suppose it would be any quicker than the train really, because I think the only airport near here is Exeter which is miles away. So come by train. Twelve o'clock from Paddington. You get out at Lapton to Nassecombe. You can do it nicely. You've got three quarters of an hour if my watch is right – though it isn't usually.'

'But where are you, Madame? What is all this *about*?'

'Greenshore House, Lapton. A car or taxi will meet you at the station at Lapton.'

'But why do you need me? What is all this *about*?' Poirot repeated frantically.

'Telephones are in such awkward places,' said Mrs. Oliver. 'This one's in the hall . . . People passing through and talking . . . I can't really hear. But I'm expecting you. Everybody will be *so* thrilled. Good bye.'

There was a sharp click as the receiver was replaced. The line hummed gently.

With a baffled air of bewilderment, Poirot put back the receiver and murmured something under his breath. Miss Lemon sat with her pencil poised, incurious. She repeated in muted tones the final phrase of dictation before the interruption.

'— allow me to assure you, my dear sir, that the hypothesis you have advanced —'

Poirot waved aside the advancement of the hypothesis.

'That was Mrs. Oliver,' he said. 'Ariadne Oliver, the detective novelist. You may have read —' But he stopped, remembering that Miss Lemon only read improving books and regarded such frivolities as fictional crime with contempt. 'She wants me to go down to Devonshire today, at once, in –' he glanced at the clock '–thirty-five minutes.'

Miss Lemon raised disapproving eyebrows.

'That will be running it rather fine,' she said. 'For what reason?'

'You may well ask! She did not tell me.'

'How very peculiar. Why not?'

'Because,' said Hercule Poirot thoughtfully, 'she was afraid of being overheard. Yes, she made that quite clear.'

'Well, really,' said Miss Lemon, bristling in her employer's defence. 'The things people expect! Fancy thinking that you'd go rushing off on some wild goose chase like that! An important man like you! I have always noticed that these artists and writers are very unbalanced – no sense of proportion. Shall I telephone through a telegram: *Regret unable leave London*?'

Her hand went out to the telephone. Poirot's voice arrested the gesture.

'*Du tout!*' he said. 'On the contrary. Be so kind as

to summon a taxi immediately.' He raised his voice. 'Georges! A few necessities of toilet in my small valise. And quickly, very quickly, I have a train to catch.'

CHAPTER TWO

THE TRAIN, having done one hundred and eighty-odd miles of its two hundred and twelve miles journey at top speed, puffed gently and apologetically through the last thirty and drew into Lapton station. Only one person alighted, Hercule Poirot. He negotiated with care a yawning gap between the step of the train and the platform and looked round him. At the far end of the train a porter was busy inside a luggage compartment. Poirot picked up his valise and walked back along the platform to the exit. He gave up his ticket and walked out through the booking office.

A large Humber saloon was drawn up outside and a chauffeur in uniform came forward.

'Mr. Hercule Poirot?' he inquired respectfully.

He took Poirot's case from him and opened the door of the car for him. They drove away from the station, over the railway bridge and down a country road which presently disclosed a very beautiful river view.

'The Dart, sir,' said the chauffeur.

'*Magnifique!*' said Poirot obligingly.

The road was a long straggling country lane running between green hedges, dipping down and then up. On the upward slope two girls in shorts with bright scarves over their heads and carrying heavy rucksacks on their backs were toiling slowly upwards.

'There's a Youth Hostel just above us, sir,' explained the chauffeur, who had clearly constituted himself Poirot's guide to Devon . . . 'Upper Greenshore, they call it. Come for a couple of nights at a time, they do, and very busy they are there just now. Forty or fifty a night.'

'Ah, yes,' said Poirot. He was reflecting, and not for the first time, that seen from the back, shorts were becoming to very few of the female sex. He shut his eyes in pain.

'They seem heavily laden,' he murmured.

'Yes, sir, and it's a long pull from the station or the bus stop. Best part of two miles. If you don't object, sir,' he hesitated, 'we could give them a lift.'

'By all means. By all means,' said Poirot benignantly.

The chauffeur slowed down and came to a purring halt beside the two girls. Two flushed and perspiring faces were raised hopefully. The door was opened and the girls climbed in.

'It is most kind, please,' said one of them politely in a foreign accent. 'It is longer way than I think, yes.' The other girl who clearly had not much English merely nodded her head several times gratefully and smiled, and murmured '*Grazie*'

Bright dark chestnut fuzzy curls escaped from her head scarf and she had on big earnest looking spectacles.

The English speaking girl continued talking vivaciously. She was in England for a fortnight's holiday. Her home was Rotterdam. She had already seen Stratford on Avon, Clovelly, Exeter Cathedral, Torquay and, 'after visiting beauty spot here and historic Dartmouth, I go to Plymouth, discovery of New World from Plymouth Hoe.'

The Italian girl murmered 'Hoe?' and shook her head, puzzled.

'She does not much English speak,' said the Dutch girl, but I understand she has relative near here married to gentleman who keeps a shop for groceries, so she will spend time with them. My friend I come from Rotterdam with has eat veal and ham pie not good in shop at Exeter and is sick there. It is not always good in hot weather, the veal and ham pie.'

The chauffeur slowed down at a fork in the road. The girls got out, uttered thanks in two languages and the chauffeur with a wave of the hand directed them to the left hand road. He also laid aside for a moment his Olympian aloofness.

'You want to be careful of Cornish Pasties too,' he warned them. Put *anything* in them, they will, holiday time.'

The car drove rapidly down the right hand road into a thick belt of trees.

'Nice enough young women, some of them, though foreign,' said the chauffeur. 'But absolutely shocking the way they trespass. Don't seem to understand places are private.'

They went on, down a steep hill through woods,

then through a gate and along a drive, winding up finally in front of a big white Georgian house looking out over the river.

The chauffeur opened the door of the car as a tall butler appeared on the steps.

'Mr. Hercule Poirot?'

'Yes.'

'Mrs. Oliver is expecting you, sir. You will find her down at the Battery. Allow me to show you the way.'

Poirot was directed to a winding path that led along the wood with glimpses of the river below. The path descended gradually until it came out at last on an open space, round in shape with a low battlemented parapet. On the parapet Mrs. Oliver was sitting.

She rose to meet him and several apples fell from her lap and rolled in all directions. Apples seemed to be an inescapable motif of meeting Mrs. Oliver.

'I can't think why I always drop things,' said Mrs. Oliver somewhat indistinctly, since her mouth was full of apple. 'How are you, M. Poirot?'

'*Très bien, chère Madame*,' replied Poirot politely. 'And you?'

Mrs. Oliver was looking somewhat different from when Poirot had last seen her, and the reason lay, as she had already hinted over the telephone, in the fact that she had once more experimented with her *coiffure*. The last time Poirot had seen her, she had been adopting a windswept effect. Today, her hair, richly blued, was piled upward in a multiplicity of rather artificial little curls in a pseudo Marquise style. The Marquise effect ended at her neck; the rest of her could have been definitely labelled 'country practical,' consisting of a violent yolk of egg rough tweed coat and skirt and a rather bilious looking mustard coloured jumper.

'I knew you'd come,' said Mrs. Oliver cheerfully.

'You could not possibly have known,' said Poirot severely.

'Oh, yes I did.'

'I still ask myself why I am here.'

'Well, I know the answer. Curiosity.'

Poirot looked at her and his eyes twinkled a little.

'Your famous Woman's Intuition,' he said, 'has perhaps for once not led you too far astray.'

'Now, don't laugh at my woman's intuition. Haven't I always spotted the murderer right away?'

Poirot was gallantly silent. Otherwise he might have replied, 'At the fifth attempt, perhaps, and not always then!'

Instead he said, looking round him, 'It is indeed a beautiful property that you have here.'

'This? But it doesn't belong to *me*, M. Poirot. Did you think it did? Oh, no, it belongs to some people called Stubbs.'

'Who are they?'

'Oh, nobody really,' said Mrs. Oliver vaguely. 'Just rich. No, I'm down here professionally, doing a job.'

'Ah, you are getting local colour for one of your *chefs-d'oeuvre*?'

'No, no. Just what I said. I'm doing a job. I've been engaged to arrange a murder.'

Poirot stared at her.

'Oh, not a real one,' said Mrs. Oliver reassuringly. 'There's a big Fête thing on tomorrow, and as a kind of novelty there's going to be a Murder Hunt. Arranged by me. Like a Treasure Hunt, you see; only they've had a Treasure Hunt so often that they thought this would be a novelty. So they offered me a very substantial fee to come down and think it up. Quite fun, really – rather a change from the usual grim routine.'

'How does it work?'

'Well, there'll be a Victim, of course. And Clues. And Suspects. All rather conventional – you know, the Vamp and the Blackmailer and the Young Lovers and the Sinister Butler and so on. Half a crown to enter and you get shown the first Clue and you've got to find the Victim, and the Weapon and say Whodunnit and the Motive. And there are Prizes.'

'Remarkable,' said Hercule Poirot.

'Actually,' said Mrs. Oliver ruefully, 'it's all much harder to arrange than you'd think. Because you've got to allow for real people being quite intelligent, and in my books they needn't be.'

'And it is to assist you in arranging this that you have sent for me?'

Poirot did not try very hard to keep an outraged resentment out of his voice.

'Oh, no,' said Mrs. Oliver. 'Of course not! I've done all that. Everything's all set for tomorrow. No, I wanted you for quite another reason.'

'What reason?'

Mrs. Oliver's hands strayed upward to her head. She was just about to sweep them frenziedly through her hair in the old familiar gesture when she remembered the intricacy of her *coiffure*. Instead, she relieved her feelings by tugging at her ear lobes.

'I daresay I'm a fool,' she said. 'But I think there's something wrong.'

'Something *wrong*? How?'

'I don't know . . . That's what I want *you* to find out. But I've felt – more and more – that I was being – oh! – *engineered* . . . jockeyed along . . . Call me a fool if you like, but I can only say that if there was to be a *real* murder tomorrow instead of a fake one, I shouldn't be surprised!'

Poirot stared at her and she looked back at him defiantly.

'Very interesting,' said Poirot.

'I suppose you think I'm a complete fool,' said Mrs. Oliver defensively.

'I have never thought you a fool,' said Poirot.

'And I know what you always say – or look – about Intuition.'

'One calls things by different names,' said Poirot. 'I am quite ready to believe that you have noticed something or heard something that has definitely aroused in you anxiety. I think it possible that you yourself may not even know just what it is that you have seen

41

or noticed or heard. You are aware only of the *result*. If I may so put it, you do not know what it is that you know. You may label that intuition if you like.'

'It makes one feel such a fool,' said Mrs. Oliver, ruefully, 'not to be able to be *definite*.'

'We shall arrive,' said Poirot encouragingly. 'You say that you have had the feeling of being – how did you put it – jockeyed along? Can you explain a little more clearly what you mean by that?'

'Well, it's rather difficult . . . You see, this is *my* murder, so to speak. I've thought it out and planned it and it all fits in – dovetails. Well, if you know anything at all about writers, you'll know that they can't stand suggestions. People say, "Splendid, but wouldn't it be better if so and so did so and so?" Or, "Wouldn't it be a wonderful idea if the victim was A instead of B? Or the murderer turned out to be D instead of E?" I mean, one wants to say: "All right then, write it yourself if you want it that way"!'

Poirot nodded.

'And that is what has been happening?'

'Not quite . . . That sort of silly suggestion has been made, and then I've flared up, and they've given in, but have just slipped in some quite minor

42

trivial suggestion and because I've made a stand over the other, I've accepted the triviality without noticing much.'

'I see,' said Poirot. 'Yes – it is a method, that . . . Something rather crude and preposterous is put forward – but that is not really the point. The small minor alteration is really the objective. Is that what you mean?'

'That's exactly what I mean,' said Mrs. Oliver. 'And, of course, I *may* be imagining it, but I don't think I am – and none of the things seem to matter anyway. But it's got me worried – that, and a sort of – well – *atmosphere*.'

'Who has made these suggestions of alterations to you?'

'Different people,' said Mrs. Oliver. 'If it was just *one* person I'd be more sure of my ground. But it's not just one person – although I think it is really. I mean it's one person working through other quite unsuspecting people.'

'Have you an idea as to who that one person is?'

Mrs. Oliver shook her head.

'It's somebody very clever and very careful,' she said. 'It might be anybody.'

'Who is there?' asked Poirot. 'The cast of characters must be fairly limited?'

'Well,' began Mrs. Oliver. 'There's Sir George Stubbs who owns this place. Rich and plebeian and frightfully stupid outside business, I should think, but probably dead sharp in it. And there's Lady Stubbs, Hattie, about twenty years younger than he is, rather beautiful, but dumb as a fish – in fact, *I* think she's definitely half-witted. Married him for his money, of course, and doesn't think about anything but clothes and jewels. Then there's Michael Weyman – he's an architect, quite young, and good looking in a craggy kind of artistic way. He's designing a tennis pavilion for Sir George and repairing the Folly.'

'Folly? What is that – a masquerade?'

'No, it's architectural. One of those little sort of temple things, white with columns. You've probably seen them at Kew. Then there's Miss Brewis, she's a sort of secretary housekeeper, who runs things and writes letters – very grim and efficient. And then there are the people round about who come in and help. A young married couple who have a cottage down by the river – Alec Legge and his wife Peggy. And Captain Warborough, who's the Mastertons' agent. And the Mastertons, of course, and old Mrs. Folliat who lives in what used to be the lodge. Her husband's people owned Greenshore originally. But they've died out or been killed in wars and there were lots of death duties so the last heir sold the place.'

'Whose idea was the Murder Hunt?'

'Mrs. Masterton's, I think. She's the local Member of Parliament's wife. She's very good at organising. She persuaded Sir George to have the Fête here. You see the place has been empty for so many years that she thinks people will be keen to pay and come in to see it.'

'That all seems straightforward enough,' said Poirot.

'It all *seems* straightforward,' said Mrs. Oliver obstinately, 'but it isn't. I tell you, M. Poirot, there's something *wrong*.'

Poirot looked at Mrs. Oliver and Mrs. Oliver looked back at Poirot.

'How have you accounted for my presence here? For your summons to me?' Poirot asked.

'That was easy,' said Mrs. Oliver. 'You're to give away the prizes. For the Murder Hunt. Everybody's awfully thrilled. I said I knew you, and could probably persuade you to come and that I was sure your name would be a terrific draw – as, of course, it will be,' Mrs. Oliver added tactfully.

'And the suggestion was accepted – without demur?'

'I tell you, everybody was thrilled.'

Mrs. Oliver thought it unnecessary to mention that amongst the younger generation one or two had asked 'Who *is* Hercule Poirot?'

'*Everybody?* Nobody spoke against the idea?'

Mrs. Oliver shook her head.

'That is a pity,' said Hercule Poirot.

'You mean it might have given us a line?'

'A would-be criminal could hardly be expected to welcome my presence.'

'I suppose you think I've imagined the whole thing,' said Mrs. Oliver ruefully. 'I must admit that until I started talking to you I hadn't realised how very little I've got to go upon.'

'Calm yourself,' said Poirot kindly. 'I am intrigued and interested. Where do we begin?'

Mrs. Oliver glanced at her watch.

'It's just tea-time. We'll go back to the house and then you can meet everybody.'

She took a different path from the one by which Poirot had come. This one seemed to lead in the opposite direction.

'We pass by the boathouse this way,' Mrs. Oliver explained.

As she spoke the boathouse came into view. It jutted out on to the river and was a picturesque thatched affair.

'That's where the Body's going to be,' said Mrs. Oliver. 'The body for the Murder Hunt, I mean.'

'And who is going to be killed?'

'Oh, a girl hiker, who is really the Yugoslavian first wife of a young Atom Scientist,' said Mrs. Oliver glibly.

Poirot blinked.

'Of course it looks as though the Atom Scientist had killed her – but naturally it's not as simple as *that*.'

'Naturally not – since *you* are concerned –'

Mrs. Oliver accepted the compliment with a wave of the hand.

'Actually,' she said, 'she's killed by the Country Squire – and the motive is really rather ingenious – I don't believe many people will get it – though there's a perfectly clear pointer in the fifth clue.'

Poirot abandoned the subtleties of Mrs. Oliver's plot to ask a practical question.

'But how do you arrange for a suitable body?'

'Girl Guide,' said Mrs. Oliver. 'Peggy Legge was going to be it – but now they want her to do the fortune teller – so it's a Girl Guide called Marlene Tucker. Rather dumb and sniffs. It's quite easy – just peasant scarves and a rucksack – and all she has to do when she hears someone coming is to flop down on the floor and arrange the cord round her neck. Rather dull for the poor kid – just sticking inside that boathouse until she's found, but I've arranged for her to have a nice bundle of comics – there's a clue to the murderer scribbled on one of them as a matter of fact – so it all works in.'

'Your ingenuity leaves me spellbound! The things you think of !'

'It's never difficult to *think* of things,' said Mrs. Oliver. 'The trouble is that you think of too many, and then it all becomes too complicated, so you have to relinquish some of them and that *is* rather agony. We'll go up this way now.'

They started up a steep zig-zagging path that led them back along the river at a higher level. At a

twist through the trees they came out on a space sur-
mounted by a small white plastered temple. Standing
back and frowning at it was a young man wearing
dilapidated flannel trousers and a shirt of rather viru-
lent green. He spun round towards them.

'Mr. Michael Weyman, M. Hercule Poirot,' said
Mrs. Oliver.

The young man acknowledged the introduction
with a careless nod.

'Extraordinary,' he said bitterly, 'the places people
put things! This thing here, for instance. Put up only
about a year ago – quite nice of its kind and quite in
keeping with the period of the house. But why *here*?
These things were meant to be seen – "situated on an
eminence" – that's how they phrased it – with a nice
grassy approach and daffodils. But here's this poor
little devil, stuck away in the midst of trees – not vis-
ible from anywhere – you'd have to cut down about
twenty trees before you'd even see it from the river.'

'Perhaps there wasn't any other place,' said Mrs.
Oliver.

Michael Weyman snorted.

'Top of that grassy bank by the house – perfect
natural setting. But no, these tycoon fellows are

all the same – no artistic sense. Has a fancy for a "Folly," as he calls it, orders one. Looks round for somewhere to put it. Then, I understand, a big oak tree crashes down in a gale. Leaves a nasty scar. "Oh, we'll tidy the place up by putting a Folly there," says the silly ass. That's all they ever think about, these rich city fellows, tidying up! I wonder he hasn't put beds of red geraniums and calceolarias all round the house! A man like that shouldn't be allowed to own a place like this!'

He sounded heated.

'This young man,' Poirot observed to himself, 'assuredly does not like Sir George Stubbs.'

'It's bedded down in concrete,' said Weyman. 'And there's loose soil underneath – so it's subsided. Cracked all up here – it will be dangerous soon. Better pull the whole thing down and re-erect it on the top of the bank near the house. That's my advice, but the obstinate old fool won't hear of it.'

'What about the tennis pavilion?' asked Mrs. Oliver.

Gloom settled even more deeply on the young man.

'He wants a kind of Chinese pagoda,' he said with a groan. 'Dragons if you please! Just because Lady

Stubbs fancies herself in Chinese coolie hats. Who'd be an architect? Anyone who wants something decent built hasn't got the money, and those who have the money want something too utterly goddam awful!'

'You have my commiserations,' said Poirot gravely.

Mrs. Oliver moved on towards the house and Poirot and the dispirited architect prepared to follow her.

'These tycoons,' said the latter, bitterly, 'can't understand first principles.' He delivered a final kick to the lopsided Folly. 'If the foundations are rotten – everything's rotten.'

'It is profound what you say there,' said Poirot. 'Yes, it is profound.'

The path they were following came out from the trees and the house showed white and beautiful before them in its setting of dark trees rising up behind it.

'It is of a veritable beauty, yes,' murmured Poirot.

'He wants to build a billiard room on,' said Mr. Weyman venomously.

On the bank below them a small elderly lady was busy with secateurs on a clump of shrubs. She climbed up to greet them, panting slightly.

'Everything neglected for years,' she said. 'And so difficult nowadays to get a man who understands shrubs. This hillside should be a blaze of colour in March and April, but very disappointing this year – all this dead wood ought to have been cut away last autumn –'

'M. Hercule Poirot, Mrs. Folliat,' said Mrs. Oliver. The elderly lady beamed.

'So this is the great M. Poirot! It *is* kind of you to come and help us tomorrow. This clever lady here has thought out a most puzzling problem – it will be such a novelty.'

Poirot was faintly puzzled by the graciousness of the little lady's manner. She might, he thought, have been his hostess.

He said politely, 'Mrs. Oliver is an old friend of mine. I was delighted to be able to respond to her request. This is indeed a beautiful spot, and what a superb and noble mansion.'

Mrs. Folliat nodded in a matter-of-fact manner.

'Yes. It was built by my husband's great-grandfather in 1790. There was an Elizabethan house previously. It fell into disrepair and burned down in about 1700. Our family has lived here since 1598.'

Her voice was calm and matter of fact. Poirot looked at her with closer attention. He saw a very small and compact little person, dressed in shabby tweeds. The most noticeable feature about her was her clear china blue eyes. Her grey hair was closely confined by a hairnet. Though obviously careless of her appearance, she had that indefinable air of being someone, which is so hard to explain.

As they walked together towards the house, Poirot said diffidently, 'It must be hard for you to have strangers living here.'

There was a moment's pause before Mrs. Folliat answered. Her voice was clear and precise and curiously devoid of emotion.

'So many things are hard, M. Poirot,' she said.

CHAPTER THREE

TEA WAS in full swing in the drawing room. Mrs. Oliver performed introductions to Sir George Stubbs, Miss Brewis, Lady Stubbs, Mrs. Masterton, Captain Warborough, Mr. and Mrs. Legge. Sir George was a big red-faced bearded man of about fifty with a loud jovial voice and manner, and shrewd pale blue eyes that did not look jovial at all. Miss Brewis who presided behind the teatray, pouring out with rapid efficiency, was forty at a guess, plain, neat and ascetic in appearance. Beside her Mrs. Masterton, a somewhat monumental woman, bayed like a bloodhound in a deep voice. Poirot even thought she looked rather like a bloodhound,

AGATHA CHRISTIE

with her full rather underhung jaw and mournful, slightly bloodshot eyes.

'You've *got* to settle this dispute about the tea tent, Jim,' she was saying. 'We can't have the whole thing a fiasco because of these silly women and their local feuds.'

Captain Warborough, who wore a check coat and had a horsey appearance, showed a lot of very white teeth in a wolfish smile.

'We'll settle it,' he said heartily. 'I'll go and talk to them like a Dutch uncle. Now about the fortune teller's tent – do you think over by the magnolia? Or at the far end up against the rhododendrons?'

Shrill controversy arose – in which young Mrs. Legge took a prominent part. She was a slim attractive blonde – her husband, Alec, had a badly sunburnt face and untidy red hair. He was obviously not a talker and only contributed an occasional monosyllable.

Poirot, having received his cup of tea from Miss Brewis, found a place by his hostess and sat down carefully balancing a cream cake on the edge of his saucer.

Lady Stubbs was sitting a little way away from the others. She was leaning back in an armchair, clearly uninterested in the conversation, gazing down appreciatively at her outspread right hand which lay on the arm of her chair. The nails were very long and varnished a deep puce. On the third finger was a very beautifully set emerald. She was turning the hand a little from left to right, so that the stone caught the light.

When Poirot spoke, she looked up in a startled, almost childlike manner.

'This is a beautiful room, Madame,' he said appreciatively.

'I suppose it is,' said Lady Stubbs vaguely. Yes, it's very nice.'

She was wearing a big coolie hat of vivid magenta straw. Beneath it her face showed the pinky reflection on its dead white surface. She was heavily made up in an exotic un-English style. Dead white matt skin, vivid almost purple lips, mascara round the eyes. Her black smooth hair fitted like a black velvet cap. It was an un-English face with all the languor of the sun behind it. But it was the eyes that startled Poirot. They seemed strangely vacant.

She said, 'Do you like my ring? George gave it to me yesterday.'

'It is a very lovely ring, Madame.'

She said: 'George gives me lots of things. He's very kind.'

She spoke with the satisfaction of a child.

Almost as though to a child, Poirot replied, 'That must make you very happy.'

'Oh yes, I'm *very* happy,' said Lady Stubbs, warmly. 'You like Devonshire?'

'I think so. It's nice in the day time. But there aren't any nightclubs.'

'Oh yes. I like the Casino, too. Why are there not any Casinos in England?'

'I have often wondered – I do not think it would accord with the English character.'

She looked at him vacantly, then frowned in a puzzled way.

'I won forty thousand francs at Monte Carlo once,' she said. 'I put it on number seven. My own money.'

'That must have been a great thrill.'

'Yes.' She looked at him solemnly. 'It wouldn't matter so much now. George is very rich.'

'Indeed, Madame?'

'Yes.' She sighed. 'They never let me have enough money of my own. I wanted so many things.' A smile curved up the painted mouth. 'George gives them all to me now.'

Then, once again, her head on one side, she watched her ring flash on her hand, and said in a confidential whisper, 'D'you see? It's *winking* at me.'

She burst out laughing and Poirot felt a slight sense of shock. It was a loud uncontrolled laugh.

'Hattie!'

It was Sir George's voice. It held very faint admonition. Lady Stubbs stopped laughing.

Poirot, turning his slightly embarrassed gaze away from his hostess, met the eyes of Captain Warborough. They were ironic and amused.

'If you've finished your tea, M. Poirot,' he said, 'perhaps you'd like to come and vet the little show we're putting on tomorrow.'

Poirot rose obediently. As he followed Captain Warborough out of the room, he saw out of the tail of his eye Mrs. Folliat cross to take the vacant chair by his hostess and saw Hattie turn eagerly towards her, with a child's welcoming affection.

'Beautiful creature, isn't she?' drawled War-borough. 'Bowled over old George Stubbs all right. Nothing's too good for her! Loads her with jewels and mink and all the rest of it. Whether he realises she's a bit wanting in the upper storey I've never discovered. I suppose with a woman as beautiful as that it doesn't really matter.'

'What nationality is she?' Poirot asked curiously.

'Comes from the West Indies or thereabouts I've always understood. A creole – I don't mean a half-caste, but one of those old intermarried familes . . . Ah, here we are, it's all set out in here.'

Poirot followed him into a room lined with book shelves. On a table by the window various impedimenta were set out.

A large pile of printed cards was at one side. Poirot took one and read:

Suspects

Estella da Costa	– a beautiful and mysterious woman
Colonel Blunt	– the local Squire
Samuel Fischer	– a blackmailer
Joan Blunt	– Colonel Blunt's daughter
Peter Gaye	– a young Atom Scientist
Miss Willing	– the housekeeper
Quiett	– a butler
Esteban Perenna	– an uninvited guest

Weapons
A length of clothes line
Tunisian dagger
Weedkiller
Bow and arrow
Army rifle
Bronze statuette

Captain Warborough explained:

'Everyone gets a notebook and pencil to copy down the clues and then on the back of your entry card you fill in your solution –'

Solution:
By whom committed?...
For what motive? ....
By what method? ....
Time and Place: ....
Reasons for arriving at your conclusions:..................
....

'The first clue's a photograph. Every starter gets one.'

Poirot took the small snapshot from him and

studied it with a frown. Then he turned it upside down. Warborough laughed.

'Ingenious bit of trick photography,' he said. 'Quite simple when you know what it is.'

'Some kind of a barred window?'

Warborough laughed.

'Looks a bit like it. No, it's a section of a tennis net.'

'Ah! Yes – I see it could be that now.'

'So much depends on how you look at it, eh?' laughed Warborough.

'As you say.' Poirot repeated the words meditatively. 'The way you look at a thing . . .'

He listened with only half his attention to Warborough's exposition of Mrs. Oliver's subtleties. When he left the library, Miss Brewis accosted him.

'Ah, there you are, M. Poirot. I want to show you your room.'

She led him up the staircase and along a passage to a big airy room looking out over the river.

'There is a bathroom just opposite. Sir George talks of adding more bathrooms, but to do so would sadly impair the proportions of the rooms. I hope you'll find everything comfortable.'

'Yes, indeed.' Poirot swept an appreciative eye

over the small bookstand, the reading lamp and the box labelled Biscuits by the bedside. 'You seem, in this house, to have everything organised to perfection. Am I to congratulate you, or my charming hostess?'

'Lady Stubbs's time is fully taken up in being charming,' said Miss Brewis, a slightly acid note in her voice.

'A very decorative young woman,' mused Poirot.

'As you say.'

'But in other respects is she not, perhaps –' he broke off. '*Pardon.* I am indiscreet. I comment on something I ought not, perhaps, to mention.'

Miss Brewis gave him a steady look. She said drily, 'Lady Stubbs knows perfectly well exactly what she is doing. Besides being, as you said, a very decorative young woman, she is also a very shrewd one.'

She had turned away and left the room before Poirot's eyebrows had fully risen in surprise. So that was what the efficient Miss Brewis thought, was it? Or had she merely said so for some reason of her own? And why had she made such a statement to him – to a newcomer? Because he *was* a newcomer, perhaps, and also because he was a foreigner? As Hercule Poirot had discovered by experience, there were many English people who considered that what one said to foreigners didn't count!

He frowned perplexedly, staring absentmindedly out of the window as he did so. Lady Stubbs came out of the house with Mrs. Folliat and they stood for a moment or two by the big magnolia tree. Then Mrs. Folliat nodded a goodbye, and trotted off down the drive. Lady Stubbs stood watching her for a moment, then absent-mindedly pulled off a magnolia flower, smelt it and began slowly to walk down the path that led through the trees to the river. She looked just once over her shoulder before she disappeared from sight. From behind the magnolia tree Michael Weyman came quietly into view, paused a moment and then followed the tall slim figure down into the trees.

A good-looking and dynamic young man, Poirot thought, with a more attractive personality, no doubt, than that of Sir George Stubbs . . .

But if so, what of it? Such patterns formed themselves eternally through life. Rich middle-aged unattractive husband, young and beautiful wife with or without sufficient mental development, attractive and susceptible young man. What was there in that to make Mrs. Oliver utter a peremptory summons through the telephone? Mrs. Oliver, no doubt, had a vivid imagination, but –

'But after all,' murmured Hercule Poirot to himself, 'I am not a consultant in adultery – or in incipient adultery.'

It occurred to him that he should, perhaps, have paid more attention to the details of Mrs. Oliver's Murder Hunt.

'The time is short – short,' he murmured to himself. As yet I know *nothing* – *Is* there something wrong here, as Mrs. Oliver believes? I am inclined to think there is. But what? Who is there who could enlighten me?'

After a moment's reflection he seized his hat (Poirot never risked going out in the evening air with uncovered head), and hurried out of his room and down the stairs. He heard afar the dictatorial baying of Mrs. Masterton's deep voice. Nearer at hand, Sir George's voice rose with an amorous intonation.

'Damned becoming that yashmak thing. Wish I had you in my harem, Peggy. I shall come and have my fortune told a good deal tomorrow. What'll you tell me, eh?'

There was a slight scuffle and Peggy Legge's voice said breathlessly, 'George, you mustn't.'

Poirot raised his eyebrows, and slipped out of a conveniently adjacent side door. He set off at top speed down a back drive which his sense of locality enabled him to predict would at some point join the front drive.

His manoeuvre was successful and enabled him – panting very slightly – to come up beside Mrs. Folliat and relieve her in a gallant manner of her gardening basket.

'You permit, Madame?'

'Oh, thank you, M. Poirot, that's very kind of you. But it's not heavy.'

'Allow me to carry it for you to your home. You live near here?'

'I actually live in the lodge by the front gate. Sir George very kindly rents it to me.'

The lodge by the front gate of her former home. How did she really feel about that, Poirot wondered.

Her composure was so absolute that he had no clue to her feelings. He changed the subject by observing:

'Lady Stubbs is much younger than her husband.'

'Twenty-three years younger, to be exact.'

'Physically she is very attractive.'

Mrs. Folliat said quietly, 'Hattie is a dear good child.'

It was not an answer he had expected. Mrs. Folliat went on:

'I know her very well, you see. For a short time she was under my care.'

'I did not know that.'

'How should you? It is in a way a sad story. Her people had estates, sugar estates, in the West Indies. As a result of an earthquake, the house there was burned down and her parents and brothers and sisters all lost their lives. Hattie herself was at a convent in Paris and was thus suddenly left without any near relatives. It was considered advisable by the executors that Hattie should be taken out in London society for a season. I accepted the charge of her.' Mrs. Folliat added with a dry smile, 'I can smarten myself up on occasions and naturally I had the necessary connections.'

'Naturally, Madame, I understand that.'

'I was going through a difficult time. My husband died just before the outbreak of war. My eldest son who was in the Navy went down with his ship, my younger son in the Army was killed in Italy. I had not very much to occupy my mind. I was left badly off. The house was put up for sale. I was glad of the distraction of having someone young to look after and take about. I became very fond of Hattie, all the more so, perhaps, because I soon realised that she was – shall we say – not fully capable of fending for herself? Understand me, M. Poirot, Hattie is *not* mentally deficient, but she is what country folk describe as "simple". She is easily imposed upon, over docile, completely open to suggestion. Fortunately there was practically no money – if she had been an heiress the position might have been one of much greater difficulty. She was attractive to men and being of an affectionate nature was easily attracted and influenced – she had to be looked after. When, after the final winding up of her parents' estate, it was discovered that the plantation was destroyed and there were more debts than assets, I could only be thankful that a man such as Sir George Stubbs had fallen in love with her and wanted to marry her.'

'Possibly – yes – it was a solution.'

'Sir George,' said Mrs. Folliat, 'though he is a self made man and – let us face it – a complete vulgarian, is both kindly and decent, besides being extremely wealthy. I don't think he would ever ask for mental companionship from a wife. Hattie is everything he wants. She displays clothes and jewels to perfection, is affectionate and willing, and is completely happy. I confess that I am very thankful that that is so, for I admit that I deliberately influenced her to accept him. If it had turned out badly –' her voice faltered a little, 'it would have been my fault for urging her to marry a man years older than herself. You see, as I told you, Hattie is completely suggestible. Anyone she is with at the time can dominate her.'

'It seems to me,' said Poirot approvingly, 'that you made there a most prudent arrangement for her. I am not, like the English, romantic. To arrange a good marriage, one must take more than romance into consideration.'

He added:

'And as for this place here, it is a most beautiful spot. Quite, as the saying goes, out of this world.'

'Since it had to be sold,' said Mrs. Folliat, 'I am glad that Sir George bought it. It was requisitioned during the war and afterwards it might have been bought and made into a guest house or a school, the rooms cut up and partitioned, distorted out of their natural beauty. Our neighbours, the Sandbournes, at Upper Greenshore, had to sell their place and it is now a Youth Hostel. One is glad that young people should enjoy themselves – and fortunately the house was late Victorian, and of no great architectural merit, so that the alterations do not matter. I'm afraid some of the young people trespass on our grounds. It makes Sir George very angry, and it's true that they have occasionally damaged the rare shrubs by hacking them about – they come through here trying to get a short cut to the Ferry across the river.'

They were standing now by the front gate. The lodge, a small white one-storeyed building, lay a little back from the drive with a small railed garden round it.

Mrs. Folliat took back her basket from Poirot with a word of thanks.

'I was always very fond of the lodge,' she said. 'Dear old Meldrum, our head gardener for thirty years, used to live there. I much prefer it to the top cottage, though that has been enlarged and modernised by Sir George. It had to be; we've got quite a young man as head gardener with a young wife – and they must have electric irons and modern cookers and all that. One must go with the times' she sighed. 'There is hardly a person left on the estate from the old days – all new faces.'

'I am glad, Madame,' said Poirot, 'that you at least have found a haven.'

'You know those lines of Spenser's? "*Sleep after toyle, port after stormie seas, ease after war, death after life, doth greatly please . . .*"'

She paused and said without any change of tone, 'It's a very wicked world, M. Poirot. And there are very wicked people in the world. You probably know that as well as I do. I don't say so before the younger people, it might discourage them, but it's true . . . Yes, it's a very wicked world . . .'

She gave him a little nod, then turned and went into the Lodge. Poirot stood still, staring at the shut door.

CHAPTER FOUR

In a mood of exploration Poirot went through the front gate and down the steep twisty road that presently emerged on a small quay. A large bell with a chain had a notice upon it to 'Ring for the Ferry.' There were various boats moored by the side of the quay. A very old man with rheumy eyes, who had been leaning against a bollard, came shuffling towards Poirot.

'Du ee want the ferry, sir?'

'I thank you, no. I have just come down from Greenshore House for a little walk.'

'Ah, 'tis up at Greenshore yu are? Worked there as a boy, I did, and my son, he was head gardner there.

But I did use to look after the boats. Old Mr. Folliat, he was fair mazed about boats. Sail in all weathers, he would. The Major, now, his son, he didn't care for sailing. Horses, that's all he cared about. And a pretty packet went on 'em. That and the bottle – had a hard time with him, his wife did. Yu've seen her, maybe – lives at the Lodge now, she du.'

'Yes, I have just left her there now.'

'Her be a Folliat, tu, second cousin from over Tiverton way. A great one for the garden, she was, all them there flowering shrubs she had put in. Even when it was took over during the war, and the two young gentlemen was gone to the war, she still looked after they shrubs and kept 'em from being over-run.'

'It was hard on her, both her sons being killed.'

'Ah, she've had a hard life, she have, what with this and that. Trouble with her husband, and trouble with the young gentlemen, tu. Not Mr. Henry. He was as nice a young gentleman as yu could wish, took after his grandfather, fond of sailing and went into the Navy as a matter of course, but Mr. James, he caused her a lot of trouble. Debts and women it were, and then, too, he were real wild in his temper. Born one of they as can't go straight. But the war suited him, as yu might say – give him his chance. Ah! There's many who can't go straight in peace who dies bravely in war.'

'So now,' said Poirot, 'there are no more Folliats at Greenshore.'

The old man's flow of talk died abruptly.

'Just as yu say, sir.'

Poirot looked curiously at the old man.

'Instead you have Sir George Stubbs. What is thought locally of him?'

'Us understands,' said the old man, 'that he be powerful rich.'

His tone sounded dry and almost amused.

'And his wife?'

'Ah, she's a fine lady from London, she is. No use for gardens, not her. They du say, too, as her du be wanting up here.'

He tapped his temple significantly.

'Not as her isn't always very nice spoken and friendly. Come here over a year ago, they did. Bought the place and had it all done up like new. I remember as though 'twere yesterday them arriving. Arrived in the evening, they did, day after the worst gale as I ever remember. Trees down right and left – one down across the drive and us had to get it sawn away in a hurry to get the drive clear. And the big oak up along, that come down and brought a lot of others down with it, made a rare mess, it did.'

'Ah, yes, where the Folly stands now?'

The old man turned aside and spat disgustedly.

'Folly 'tis called and Folly 'tis – new-fangled nonsense. Never was no Folly in the old Folliats' time. Her ladyship's idea that Folly was. Put up not three weeks after they first come, and I've no doubt she talked Sir George into it. Rare silly it looks stuck up there among the trees, like a heathen temple. A nice summerhouse now, made rustic like with stained glass – I'd have nothing against that.'

Poirot smiled faintly.

'The London ladies,' he said, 'they must have their fancies. It is sad that the day of the Folliats is over.'

'Don't ee never believe that, sir.' The old man gave a wheezy chuckle. 'Always be Folliats at Greenshore.'

'But the house belongs to Sir George Stubbs.'

'That's as may be – but there's still a Folliat here. Rare and cunning the Folliats are!'

'What do you mean?'

The old man gave him a sly sideways glance.

'Mrs. Folliat be living up tu Lodge, bain't she?' he demanded.

'Yes,' said Poirot slowly. 'Mrs. Folliat is living at the Lodge and the world is very wicked, and all the people in it are very wicked.'

The old man stared at him.

'Ah,' he said. 'Yu've got something there, maybe.'

He shuffled away again.

'But what have I got?' Poirot asked himself with irritation as he slowly walked up the hill back to the house.

CHAPTER FIVE

POIROT CAME down to breakfast on the following morning at nine-thirty. Breakfast was served in pre-war fashion. A row of hot dishes on an electric heater. Sir George was eating a full-sized Englishman's breakfast of scrambled eggs, bacon and kidneys. Mrs. Oliver and Miss Brewis had a modified version of the same. Michael Weyman was eating a plateful of cold ham. Only Lady Stubbs was unheedful of the fleshpots and was nibbling thin toast and sipping black coffee.

The post had just arrived. Miss Brewis had an enormous pile of letters in front of her which she was rapidly sorting into piles. Any of Sir George's marked *Personal* she passed over to him. The others she opened and sorted into categories.

Lady Stubbs had three letters. She opened what were clearly a couple of bills and tossed them aside. Then she opened the third letter and said suddenly and clearly, 'Oh!'

The exclamation was so startled that all heads turned towards her.

'It's from Paul,' she said. 'My cousin Paul. He's coming here in a yacht.'

'Let's see, Hattie.' Sir George held out his hand. She passed the letter down the table. He smoothed out the sheet and read.

'Who's this Paul Lopez? A cousin, you say?'

'I think so. A second cousin. I do not remember him very well – hardly at all. He was –'

'Yes, my dear?'

She shrugged her shoulders.

'It does not matter. It is all a long time ago. I was a little girl.'

'I suppose you wouldn't remember him very well. But we must make him welcome, of course,' said Sir George heartily. 'Pity in a way it's the Fête today, but we'll ask him to dinner. Perhaps we could put him up for a night or two – show him something of the country?'

Sir George was being the hearty country squire.

Lady Stubbs said nothing. She stared down into her coffee cup.

Conversation on the inevitable subject of the Fête became general. Only Poirot remained detached, watching the slim exotic figure at the head of the table. He wondered just what was going on in her mind. At that very moment her eyes came up and cast a swift glance along the table to where he sat. It was a look so shrewd and appraising that he was startled. As their eyes met, the shrewd expression vanished – emptiness returned. But that other look had been there, cold, calculating, watchful . . .

Or had he imagined it? In any case, wasn't it true that people who were slightly mentally deficient very often had a kind of sly native cunning that sometimes surprised even the people who knew them best?

He thought to himself that Lady Stubbs was certainly an enigma. People seemed to hold diametrically opposite ideas about her. Miss Brewis had intimated that Lady Stubbs knew very well what she was doing. Yet Mrs. Oliver definitely thought her halfwitted, and Mrs. Folliat who had known her long and intimately had spoken of her as someone not quite normal, who needed care and watchfulness.

Miss Brewis was probably prejudiced. She disliked Lady Stubbs for her indolence and her aloofness. Poirot wondered if Miss Brewis had been Sir George's secretary prior to his marriage. If so, she might easily resent the coming of the new regime.

Poirot himself would have agreed wholeheartedly with Mrs. Folliat and Mrs. Oliver – until this morning. And, after all, could he really rely on what had been only a fleeting impression?

Lady Stubbs got up abruptly from the table.

'I have a headache,' she said. 'I shall go and lie down in my room.'

Sir George sprang up anxiously.

'My dear girl. You're all right, aren't you?'

'It's just a headache.'

'You'll be fit enough for this afternoon, won't you?'

'Yes – I think so.'

'Take some aspirin, Lady Stubbs,' said Miss Brewis briskly. 'Have you got some or shall I bring it to you?'

'I've got some.'

She moved towards the door. As she went she dropped the handkerchief she had been holding. Poirot, moving quietly forward, picked it up unobtrusively.

Sir George, about to follow his wife, was stopped by Miss Brewis.

'About the parking of cars this afternoon, Sir George. I'm just going to give Mitchell instructions. Do you think that the best plan would be, as you said –?'

Poirot, going out of the room, heard no more.

He caught up his hostess on the stairs.

'Madame, you dropped this.'

He proffered the handkerchief with a bow.

She took it unheedingly.

'Did I? Thank you.'

'I am most distressed, Madame, that you should be suffering. Particularly when your cousin is coming.'

She answered quickly, almost violently.

'I don't want to see Paul. I don't like him. He's bad. He was always bad. I'm afraid of him. He does bad things.'

The door of the dining-room opened and Sir George came across the hall and up the stairs.

'Hattie, my poor darling. Let me come and tuck you up.'

They went up the stairs together, his arm round her tenderly, his face worried and absorbed.

Poirot looked up after them, then turned to encounter Miss Brewis moving fast, and clasping papers.

'Lady Stubbs' headache –' he began.

'No more headache than my foot,' said Miss Brewis crossly, and disappeared into her office, closing the door behind her.

Poirot sighed and passed through the front door on to the terrace. Mrs. Masterton had just driven up in a small car and was directing the elevation of a tea marquee, baying out orders in rich full-blooded tones.

She turned to greet Poirot.

'Such a nuisance, these affairs,' she observed. 'And they will always put everything in the wrong place. No – Rogers! More to the left – *left* – not right! What do you think of the weather, M. Poirot? Looks doubtful to me. Rain, of course, would spoil everything. And we've had such a fine summer this year

84

for a change. Where's Sir George? I want to talk to him about car parking.'

'His wife had a headache and has gone to lie down.'

'She'll be all right this afternoon,' said Mrs. Masterton, confidently. 'Likes functions, you know. She'll enjoy getting ready and be as pleased about it as a child. Just fetch me a bundle of those pegs over there, will you? I want to mark the places for the clock golf numbers.'

Poirot, thus pressed into service, was worked by Mrs. Masterton relentlessly, as a useful apprentice. She condescended to talk to him in the intervals of hard labour.

'Got to do everything yourself, I find. Only way . . .By the way, you're a friend of the Eliots, I believe?'

Poirot, after his long sojourn in England, comprehended that this was an indication of social recognition. Mrs. Masterton was in fact saying: 'Although a foreigner, I understand you are One of Us.' She continued to chat in an intimate manner.

'Nice to have Greenshore lived in again. We were all so afraid it was going to be a Hotel. You know what it is nowadays; one drives through the country and passes place after place with the board up "Guest House" or

"Private Hotel" or "Hotel A.A. Fully Licensed." All the houses one stayed in as a girl – or where one went to dances. Very sad. Yes, I'm glad about Greenshore and so is poor dear Amy Folliat, of course. She's had such a hard life – but never complains, I will say. Sir George has done wonders for Greenshore – and *not* vulgarised it. Don't know whether that's the result of Amy Folliat's influence – or whether it's his own natural good taste. He *has* got quite good taste, you know. Very surprising in a man like that.'

'He is not, I understand, one of the landed gentry?' said Poirot cautiously.

'He isn't even really Sir George – was christened it, I understand. Took the idea from Lord George Sanger's Circus, I suspect. Very amusing really. Of course we never let on. Rich men must be allowed their little snobberies, don't you agree? The funny thing is that in spite of his origins George Stubbs would go down perfectly well anywhere. Pure type of the eighteenth-century country squire. Good blood in him, I'd say. Father a gent and mother a barmaid, very likely.'

Mrs. Masterton interrupted herself to yell to a gardener.

'Not by that rhododendron. You must leave room for the skittles over to the right. *Right* – not left!'

She went on:

'The Brewis woman is efficient. Doesn't like poor Hattie, though. Looks at her sometimes as though she'd like to murder her. So many of these good secretaries are in love with their boss. Now where do you think Jim Warborough can have got to? Silly the way he sticks to "Captain". Not a regular soldier and never within miles of a German. One has to put up, of course, with what one can get these days – and he's a hard worker – but I feel there's something rather fishy about him. Ah! Here are the Legges.'

Peggy Legge, dressed in slacks and a yellow pullover, said brightly:

'We've come to help.'

'Lots to do,' boomed Mrs. Masterton. 'Now, let me see –'

Poirot, profiting by her inattention, slipped away. As he came round the corner of the house on to the front terrace he became a spectator of a new drama.

Two young women, in shorts, with bright blouses, had come out from the wood and were standing uncertainly looking up at the house. From the window of Lady Stubbs' bedroom Sir George leaned out and addressed them wrathfully.

'You're trespassing,' he shouted.

'Please?' said the young woman with the green headscarf.

'You can't come through here. Private.'

The other young woman, who had a royal blue headscarf, said brightly:

'Please? Greenshore Quay –' she pronounced it carefully, 'it is this way? Please.'

'You're trespassing,' bellowed Sir George.

'Please?'

'*Trespassing!* No way through. You've got to go back. *BACK!* The way you came.'

They stared as he gesticulated. Then they consulted together in a flood of foreign speech. Finally, doubtfully, blue-scarf said, 'Back? To Hostel?'

'That's right. And you take the road – *road* – round that way.'

They retreated unwillingly. Sir George mopped his brow and looked down at Poirot.

'Spend my time turning people off,' he said. 'Used to come through the top gate. I've padlocked that. Now they come through the woods, over the fence.

Think they can get down to the shore and the quay easily this way. Well, they can, of course, much quicker. But there's no right of way – never has been. And they're practically all foreigners – don't understand what you say, and just jabber back at you in Dutch or something.'

'One is Dutch and the other Italian. I saw them on their way from the station yesterday.'

'Every kind of language they talk – Yes, Hattie? What did you say?' He drew back into the room.

Poirot turned to find Mrs. Oliver and a well-developed girl of fourteen dressed in Guides' uniform close beside him.

'This is Marlene,' said Mrs. Oliver.

Marlene acknowledged the introduction with a pronounced snuffle. Poirot bowed politely

'She's the Victim,' said Mrs. Oliver.

Marlene giggled.

'I'm the horrible Corpse,' she said. 'But I'm not going to have any blood on me.' Her tone expressed disappointment.

'No?'

'No. Just strangled with a cord, that's all. I'd of *liked* to be stabbed – and have lashings of red paint.'

'Captain Warborough thought it might look too realistic,' said Mrs. Oliver.

'In a murder I think you *ought* to have blood,' said Marlene sulkily. She looked at Poirot with hungry interest. 'Seen lots of murders, haven't you? So *she* says.'

'One or two,' said Poirot modestly.

He observed with alarm that Mrs. Oliver was leaving them.

'Any sex maniacs?' asked Marlene with avidity.

'Certainly not.'

'I like sex maniacs,' said Marlene with relish. 'Reading about them, I mean.'

'You would probably not like meeting one.'

'Oh, I dunno. D'you know what? I believe we've got a sex maniac round here. My granddad saw a body in the woods once. He was scared and ran away, and when he come back it was gone. It was a woman's body. But of course he's batty, my grand-dad is, so no one listens to what he says.'

Poirot managed to escape and, regaining the house by a circuitous route, took refuge in his bedroom.

CHAPTER SIX

LUNCH WAS an early and quickly snatched affair of a cold buffet. At 2.30 a minor film star was to open the Fête. The weather, after looking ominously like rain, began to improve. By three o'clock the Fête was in full swing. People were paying the admission charge of half a crown in large numbers, and cars were lining one side of the long drive. Students from the Youth Hostel arrived in batches conversing loudly in foreign tongues. True to Mrs. Masterton's forecast, Lady Stubbs had emerged from her bedroom just before half-past two, dressed in a cyclamen dress with an enormous coolie shaped hat of black straw. She wore large quantities of diamonds.

Miss Brewis murmured sardonically, 'Thinks it's the Royal Enclosure at Ascot, evidently!'

But Poirot complimented her gravely.

'It is a beautiful creation that you have on, Madame.'

'It is nice, isn't it,' said Hattie happily. 'I wore it for Ascot.'

The minor film star was arriving and Hattie moved forward to greet her.

Poirot retreated into the background. He wandered around disconsolately – everything seemed to be proceeding in the normal fashion of Fêtes. There was a coconut shy, presided over by Sir George in his heartiest fashion. There were various 'stalls' displaying local produce of fruit, vegetables, jams and cakes – and others displaying 'fancy objects.' There were various 'raffles' going on, and a 'lucky dip' for children.

There was a good crowd of people by now and an exhibition of children's dancing began. Poirot saw no sign of Mrs. Oliver, but Lady Stubbs' cyclamen pink figure showed up amongst the crowd as she drifted rather vaguely about. The focus of attention, however, seemed to be Mrs. Folliat. She was quite transformed in appearance – wearing a hydrangea-blue foulard frock and a smart grey hat, she appeared to preside over the proceedings, greeting new arrivals, directing people to the various side shows, gracious and welcoming in manner, she was, very definitely, Mrs. Folliat of Greenshore House.

Poirot wondered whether she herself realised how completely she had slipped into the role of hostess or whether it was entirely unconscious.

He was standing by the tent labelled *'Madame Esmeralda will tell your fortune for 2/6'*. Teas had just begun to be served and there was no longer a queue for the Fortune Telling. Poirot bowed his head, entered the tent and paid over his half crown willingly for the privilege of sinking into a chair and resting his aching feet.

Madame Esmeralda was wearing flowing black robes, a scarf wound round her head and a veil across the lower half of her face which slightly muffled her remarks.

Seizing Poirot's hand she gave him a rapid reading, full of money to come, success with a dark beauty and a miraculous escape from an accident.

'It is very agreeable all that you tell me, Madame Legge. I only wish that it could come true.'

'Oh!' said Peggy. 'So you know me, do you?'

'I had advance information – Mrs. Oliver told me that you were originally to be the "Victim," but that you had been snatched from her for the "Occult".'

'I wish I *was* being the "Body,"' said Peggy. 'Much more peaceful. All Jim Warborough's fault. Is it four o'clock yet? I want my tea. I'm off duty from four to half-past.'

'Ten minutes to go, still,' said Poirot, consulting his large old-fashioned watch. 'Shall I bring you a cup of tea here?'

'No, no. I want the break – only ten minutes to go.'

Poirot emerged from the tent and was immediately challenged to guess the weight of a cake.

A Hoop-La stall presided over by a fat motherly woman urged him to try his luck and, much to his discomfiture, he immediately won a large Kewpie doll. Walking sheepishly along with this he encountered Michael Weyman who was standing gloomily on the outskirts near the top of a path that led down to the quay.

'You seem to have been enjoying yourself, M. Poirot,' he said, with a sardonic grin.

Poirot contemplated his prize.

'It is truly horrible, is it not?' he said sadly.

A small child near him suddenly burst out crying.

Poirot stooped swiftly and tucked the doll into the child's arm.

'*Voilà*, it is for you.'

The tears ceased abruptly.

'There – Violet – isn't the gentleman kind? Say, Ta, ever so –'

'Children's Fancy Dress,' called out Captain Warborough through a megaphone. 'First class – 3 to 5. Form up, please.'

He came towards them, looking from left to right.

'Where's Lady Stubbs? Anyone seen Lady Stubbs? She's supposed to be judging this.'

'I saw her about a quarter of an hour ago,' said Poirot.

'She was going in to the Fortune Teller when I saw her,' said Weyman. 'She may be still there.'

He strode across to the tent, pulled aside the flap, looked in and shook his head.

'Curse the woman!' said Warborough angrily. 'Where can she have disappeared to? The children are waiting. Perhaps she's in the house.'

He strode off rapidly.

Poirot watched him go, and then turned his head as he heard a movement behind him.

A young man was coming up the path from the Quay, a very dark young man, faultlessly attired in yachting costume. He paused as though disconcerted by the scene before him.

Then he spoke hesitatingly to Poirot.

'You will excuse me. Is this the house of Sir George Stubbs?'

'It is indeed. Are you, perhaps, the cousin of Lady Stubbs?'

'I am Paul Lopez.'

'My name is Hercule Poirot.'

They bowed to each other. Poirot explained the circumstances of the Fête. As he finished, Sir George came across the lawn towards them from the coconut shy.

'Paul Lopez? Delighted to see you. Hattie got your letter this morning. Where's your yacht?'

'It is moored at Dartmouth. I came up the river to the Quay here in my launch.'

'We must find Hattie. She's somewhere about . . . You'll dine with us this evening, I hope?'

'You are most kind.'

'Can we put you up?'

'That also is most kind, but I will sleep on my yacht. It is easier so.'

'Are you staying here long?'

'Two or three days, perhaps. It depends.' Paul Lopez shrugged elegant shoulders.

'Hattie will be delighted, I'm sure. Where *is* she? I saw her not long ago.'

He looked round in a perplexed manner.

'She ought to be judging the children's fancy dress. I can't understand it. Excuse me a moment. I'll ask Miss Brewis.'

He hurried off. Paul Lopez looked after him. Poirot looked at Paul Lopez.

'It is some little time since you last saw your cousin?' he asked.

The other shrugged his shoulders.

'I have not seen her since she was fifteen years old. Soon after that she was sent abroad – to school at a convent in France. As a child she promised to have good looks.'

He looked enquiringly at Poirot.

'She is a beautiful woman,' said Poirot.

'And that is her husband? He seems what they call "a good fellow", but not perhaps very polished? Still, for Hattie it might be perhaps a little difficult to find a suitable husband.'

Poirot remained with a politely inquiring expression on his face. The other laughed.

'Oh, it is no secret. At fifteen Hattie was mentally undeveloped. Feeble-minded, do you not call it? She is still the same?'

'It would seem so – yes,' said Poirot cautiously.

Lopez shrugged his shoulders.

'Ah well! Why should one ask it of women – that they should be intelligent? It is not necessary.'

Sir George was back, fuming, Miss Brewis with him, speaking rather breathlessly.

'I've no idea where she is, Sir George. I saw her over by the fortune teller's tent last. But that was at least twenty minutes ago. She's not in the house.'

'Is it not possible,' asked Poirot, 'that she has gone to observe the progress of Mrs. Oliver's Murder Hunt?'

Sir George's brow cleared.

'That's probably it. Look here, I can't leave the shows here. I'm in charge. Could you possibly have a look round, Poirot? You know the course.'

But Poirot did not know the course. However, an inquiry of Miss Brewis gave him rough guidance. Miss Brewis took charge of Paul Lopez and Poirot went off murmuring to himself, 'Tennis Court, Camellia Garden, The Folly, Upper Nursery Garden, Boathouse . . .'

As he passed the Coconut Shy he was amused to notice Sir George proffering wooden balls with a dazzling smile of welcome to the same two young women whom he had driven off that morning and who were clearly puzzled at his change of attitude. The fact that this morning they had been trespassers and that this afternoon they were by reason of the payment of two shillings and sixpence legally entitled to the full enjoyment of the grounds of Greenshore House was quite beyond them. They resisted the coconuts and went on to the Bran Tub.

The Dutch girl recognised Poirot and greeted him politely. Both girls had their rucksacks strapped on their shoulders and were perspiring heavily.

'My friend she goes by the 5 o'clock bus from the gate here to Torquay,' explained the Dutch girl, 'and I go across the Ferry and take the bus to Dartmouth at 6 o'clock.'

'You lead a strenuous life,' said Poirot.

'There is much to see and our time is short here.'

Poirot bowed gratefully and went on his way to the Tennis Court. There he drew a blank. He went on to the Camellia Garden.

In the Camellia Garden Poirot found Mrs. Oliver dressed in purple splendour, sitting on a garden seat in a brooding attitude, looking rather like Mrs. Siddons. She beckoned him to the seat beside her.

'This is only the second Clue,' she hissed. 'I think I've made them too difficult. Nobody's come yet.'

At this moment a young man in shorts, with a prominent Adam's apple, entered the garden. With a cry of satisfaction he hurried to a tree in one corner and a further satisfied cry announced his discovery of the next clue. Passing them, he felt impelled to communicate his satisfaction.

'Lots of people don't know about cork trees,' he said, holding out a small cork. 'There's a whole box of them under the tennis net. Clever photograph, but I spotted what it was. This clue will make 'em go looking for a bottle of some kind. Very delicate, cork trees, only hardy in this part of the world. I'm interested in rare shrubs and trees. Now where does one go, I wonder?'

He frowned over the entry in the notebook he carried.

'I've copied the next clue but it doesn't seem to make sense.' He eyed them suspiciously. 'You competing?'

'Oh, no,' said Mrs. Oliver. 'We're just – looking on.'

'Righty-ho . . . "*When lovely woman stoops to folly*" . . . I've an idea I've heard that somewhere.'

'It is a well-known quotation,' said Poirot.

'A Folly can also be a building,' said Mrs. Oliver, helpfully. 'White – with pillars,' she added.

'*That's* an idea! Thanks a lot. They say Mrs. Ariadne Oliver is down here herself somewhere about. I'd like to get her autograph. You haven't seen her about, have you?'

'No,' said Mrs. Oliver firmly.

'I'd like to meet her. Good yarns she writes.' He lowered his voice. 'But they say she drinks like a fish.'

He hurried off and Mrs. Oliver said indignantly, 'Really! That's most unfair when I only like lemonade!'

'And have you not just perpetrated the greatest unfairness in helping that young man towards the next clue?'

'Considering he's the only one who's got here so far, I thought he ought to be encouraged.'

'But you wouldn't give him your autograph.'

'That's different,' said Mrs. Oliver. 'Sh! Here come some more.'

But these were not clue hunters. They were two women who having paid for admittance were determined to get their money's worth by seeing the grounds thoroughly.

They were hot and dissatisfied.

'You'd think they'd have *some* nice flower beds,' said one to the other. 'Nothing but trees and more trees. It's not what I call a *garden*.'

Mrs. Oliver nudged Poirot, and they slipped quietly away.

'Supposing,' said Mrs. Oliver distractedly, 'that *nobody* ever finds my body?'

'Patience, Madame, and courage,' said Poirot. 'The afternoon is still young.'

'That's true,' said Mrs. Oliver, brightening. 'And it's half price admission after four-thirty, so probably lots of people will flock in. Let's go and see how that Marlene child is getting on. I don't really trust that girl, you know. No sense of responsibility. I wouldn't put it past her to sneak away quietly, instead of being a corpse, and go and have tea. You know what people are like about their teas.'

They proceeded amicably along the woodland path and Poirot commented on the geography of the property.

'I find it very confusing,' he said. 'So many paths, and one is never sure where they lead. And trees, trees everywhere.'

'You sound like that disgruntled woman we've just left.'

They passed the Folly and zigzagged down the path to the river. The outlines of the boathouse showed beneath them.

Poirot remarked that it would be awkward if the Murder searchers were to light upon the boathouse and find the body by accident.

'A sort of short cut? I thought of that. That's why the last clue is just a key. You can't unlock the door without it. It's a Yale. You can only open it from the inside.'

A short steep slope led down to the door of the boathouse which was built out over the storage space for boats. Mrs. Oliver took a key from a pocket concealed amongst her purple folds and unlocked the door.

'We've just come to cheer you up, Marlene,' she said brightly as she entered.

She felt slightly remorseful at her unjust suspicions of Marlene's loyalty, for Marlene, artistically arranged as 'the body,' was playing her part nobly, sprawled on the floor by the window.

Marlene made no response. She lay quite motionless. The wind blowing gently through the open window rustled a pile of 'Comics' spread out on the table.

'It's all right,' said Mrs. Oliver impatiently. 'It's only me and M. Poirot. Nobody's got any distance with the clues yet.'

Poirot was frowning. Very gently he pushed Mrs. Oliver aside and went and bent over the girl on the floor. A suppressed exclamation came from his lips. He looked up at Mrs. Oliver.

'So –' he said. 'That which you expected has happened.'

'You don't mean – ' Mrs. Oliver's eyes widened in horror. She grasped for one of the basket chairs and sat down. 'You can't mean – She isn't *dead*?'

Poirot nodded.

'Oh, yes,' he said. 'She is dead. Though not very long dead.'

'But how –?'

He lifted the corner of the gay scarf bound round the girl's head, so that Mrs. Oliver could see the ends of the clothes line.

'Just like *my* murder,' said Mrs. Oliver unsteadily. 'But *who*? And *why*?'

'That is the question,' said Poirot.

He forebore to add that those had also been her questions.

And that the answers to them could not be her answers, since the victim was not the Yugoslavian first wife of an Atom Scientist, but Marlene Tucker, a fourteen-year-old village girl who, as far as was known, had not an enemy in the world.

CHAPTER SEVEN

'I CAN HARDLY bear to think of it, M. Poirot,' said Mrs. Folliat.

She was sitting with him in the small morning room at Greenshore House some three hours later.

Sir George was with a couple of detective officers in the library.

'A girl whom I'm sure had never done any harm to anybody,' said Mrs. Folliat. 'But why – that's what I can't understand. Why?'

Her nice smiling elderly face seemed to have aged ten years. Her fingers clasped and unclasped a small lace handkerchief.

Poirot had been struck by her appearance and

authority earlier that day. He was struck now by the sudden collapse of this poise, by her very real and almost exaggerated distress. He wondered what it was that Mrs. Folliat knew and he did not.

'As you said to me only yesterday, Madame, it is a very wicked world.'

'Did I say that? It's true – I'm only just beginning to know how true it is . . . But believe me, M. Poirot, I never dreamed that *this* would happen . . .'

He looked at her curiously.

'Lady Stubbs, this morning –'

She interrupted him vehemently.

'Don't speak of her to me. Don't speak of her, I don't want to think of her.'

'She too spoke of wickedness.'

Mrs. Folliat seemed startled.

'What did she say?'

'She said of her cousin Paul Lopez that he was wicked – that he was a bad man and that she was afraid of him.'

'Paul Lopez? You mean that rather handsome dark young man who was here this afternoon?'

'Yes.'

Mrs. Folliat said impatiently:

'Pay no attention. Hattie is – like a child. Wicked and good – she uses those terms like a child does. Where can she be? What can have happened to her? I hope – oh! How I hope that she will never come back!'

Poirot was startled by her vehemence. The events of the afternoon made no sense whatever as far as he could see. From four o'clock no one had set eyes on Lady Stubbs. Since about then, the house and the grounds had been thoroughly searched. The police were now searching farther afield. Word had gone out to the railway stations, to the police cars patrolling the district to neighbouring towns, to hotels and guest houses in the vicinity –

Mrs. Folliat in a dry voice put the question that nobody had as yet asked in words.

'Do they think,' she said, 'that Hattie did it? Killed that child? And then ran away?'

'One does not know what they think.'

'Do *you* think so?'

'Madame, in all things there must be a pattern. As yet I cannot see a pattern. What do you think yourself? You know her very well –'

As she did not answer, he added:

'You are fond of her.'

'I was very fond of Hattie – very fond indeed.'

'You use the past tense, I notice.'

'You don't understand.'

'You believe, perhaps, that Lady Stubbs is dead?'

Mrs. Folliat stared straight in front of her. Then she said in a voice that was little more than a whisper.

'It would be better if she were dead – so much better.'

'I think perhaps I understand you. She was mentally subnormal. Her cousin mentioned it casually this afternoon. Such people are not always accountable for their actions. A sudden fit of rage –'

But Mrs. Folliat turned on him angrily.

'Hattie was never like that. She was a gentle warm-hearted girl. She would never have killed anyone.'

Poirot looked at her in some perplexity. He patched together certain fragments in his mind. Hadn't there been something a little theatrical about the sudden arrival of Lopez today? And Hattie's reaction to it – the calculating glance, the strongly expressed words of fear and dislike. He thought that he would like to know a little more about Paul Lopez. What part did Lopez play in all this? If Hattie Stubbs was dead – if she had been killed – and if in some way Marlene

Tucker had been a witness to the killing . . . Then
Marlene too would have been silenced . . .

Sir George Stubbs came into the room.

'Detective Inspector Bland would like to see you
in the library, M. Poirot,' he said.

Poirot got up and went across to the library.

Constable Hoskins who had been first on the
scene, sat at a table by the wall. He had now been
joined by Inspector Bland. The latter, speaking in soft
pleasant Devon voice, greeted Poirot with a mention
of mutual friend Superintendent Scott.

'He's an old buddy of mine, M. Poirot, and he's
often spoken to me about you. I feel I know you
quite well.'

They spoke for a moment of the Superintendent
and then Bland went on.

'I hope you can give us some help over this business, M. Poirot. We're very much in the dark. You're
staying in the house, I understand? Is there – forgive
me for asking – any special reason for that?'

'Not of the kind you mean. I am not here, that is
to say professionally. Mrs. Ariadne Oliver, the detective novelist, was commissioned to devise a Murder
Hunt for the Fête today, and being an old friend of

mine, she suggested that I should be asked to present the prize for the best solution.'

'I see. But since you've been staying in this house you've had the opportunity of observing people.'

'For a very short time,' Poirot pointed out.

'Nevertheless you can perhaps tell us certain things we would be glad to know. To begin with, what were the relations between Sir George Stubbs and his wife?'

'Excellent, I should say.'

'No disagreements, quarrels? Signs of nervous strain?'

'I shouldn't say so. Sir George appeared to be devoted to his wife and she to him.'

'No reason, therefore, for her to walk out on him?'

'I should have said, no reason whatever.'

'In fact, you think it unlikely?' the Inspector pressed him.

'I would never say that anything a woman does is unlikely, said Poirot cautiously. 'Women have curious reasons for the things they do which cannot be appreciated by us. I will admit that it seems an odd time to choose – in the middle of a Fête. Lady Stubbs was wearing Ascot clothes and very high heels.'

'There's been no indication of – another man?'

Poirot hesitated for a moment before he spoke.

'There is a young man here, Michael Weyman, an architect. He was attracted to her – definitely, I should say. And she knew it.'

'Was she attracted by him?'

'She may have been. I do not really think so.'

'He's still here, at any rate,' said Bland. 'And worried to death about what's happened to her – unless he's a better actor than I think. As far as that goes, they're all worried – not unnaturally. Let's have it frankly – *was she homicidal, M. Poirot?*'

'I should not have said so – And Mrs. Folliat who knows her well stoutly denies it.'

Constable Hoskins spoke unexpectedly.

'Tis well known hereabouts as she's queer in the head – Not all there, is the way I'd put it. Funny kind of laugh she had.'

Bland rubbed his forehead in a worried manner.

'These feeble-minded people,' he said. 'They *seem* all right – perfectly good natured – but some little thing may set them off. Supposing that she thought she saw the devil in Marlene Tucker's eyes – oh! I know that sounds fantastic, but there was a case like that in North Devon not very long ago. A woman was convinced that it was her duty to destroy evil! Lady Stubbs may have killed this girl for some balmy reason of her own. Then when she came to herself, she may have realised what she'd done and gone down to the river and drowned herself.'

Poirot was silent. His mind had wandered away from the Inspector's words. He was hearing again the voice in which Mrs. Folliat had said yesterday that it was a wicked world and that there were very wicked people in it. Supposing that it was *Mrs. Folliat* who had seen evil in Marlene Tucker . . . supposing that it was *Mrs. Folliat* who had felt divinely inspired to tighten a cord and choke the devil in Marlene Tucker . . . And Hattie Stubbs, seeking to avoid her unwanted cousin, came to the boathouse and found Mrs. Folliat with Marlene's dead body. However fond Hattie had been of Mrs. Folliat, nobody with Hattie's mentality could be relied upon to keep silence. So what then? Had Mrs. Folliat managed to silence Hattie too? But if so, where was Hattie's body? Frail little Mrs. Folliat could hardly have disposed of it without help.

It came back to the same finding:

Where was Hattie Stubbs?

Inspector Bland said frowning:

'It seems as though the two things have *got* to tie up – the murder and the disappearance. They can't be two entirely unrelated happenings – especially as there seems no reason for Lady Stubbs suddenly going off like that –'

The lady might have just wandered away, seeing as she's balmy,' the Constable offered.

'There would have to be some reason,' said Bland obstinately.

He looked inquiringly at Poirot.

'You can't suggest anything, M. Poirot?'

'She was startled and upset at breakfast this morning when she received a letter saying Mr. Lopez was coming here today.'

Bland raised his eyebrows.

'But he'd written to her before he left the West Indies – saying that he was coming to England.'

'Is that what he told you?'

'That's what he said, yes.'

Poirot shook his head.

'Either he is lying – or else that letter of his was suppressed. Lady Stubbs did not receive it. Both she

and Sir George appeared completely taken by surprise this morning.'

'And was she upset?'

'She was very upset. She told me that her cousin
was a bad man and did bad things, and that she was
afraid of him.'

'She was afraid of him – eh?'

Bland considered the point.

'Lopez has been thoroughly co-operative,' he
said. 'He's what I call the smarmy type – one doesn't
know what he's really thinking, but he was most
polite. We called upon him on his yacht and he went
out of his way to insist we looked over it. He assured
us that Lady Stubbs had not come to the yacht, and
that he hadn't seen her at all.'

'As far as I know, that is the truth,' said Poirot.

'When Lopez arrived at the Fête, Lady Stubbs had
already disappeared.'

'If she didn't want to meet him, she could have
easily gone to her room, and pleaded a headache.'

'Easily.'

'So it was more than not just wanting to meet him
. . . To run away, she must really have feared him
very much.'

'Yes.'

'And that puts Lopez in a more sinister light . . . Still – if she's only run away, we're bound to pick her up before long. I can't understand why we haven't already done so . . .'

Unspoken, there hovered between them an implication of a more sinister possibility . . .

'To go back to the murdered girl,' said Poirot. 'You have questioned her family? They can suggest no reason for the crime?'

'Nothing whatever.'

'She had not been –' Poirot paused delicately.

'No, no, nothing of that kind.'

'I am glad.' Poirot was remembering Marlene's remarks about sex maniacs.

'Hadn't even got a boy friend,' said the Inspector.

'Or so her people say. Probably true enough – the things she scribbled on those Comics show a bit of wishful thinking.'

He gestured towards the pile of Comics that Poirot had last seen in the boathouse and which were now reposing at the Inspector's elbow.

Poirot asked: 'You permit?' and Bland nodded.

Poirot ran rapidly through the sheets. In a straggling

childish hand, Marlene had scrawled her comments on life.

'Jackie Blake goes with Susan Barnes.' 'Peter pinches girls at the pictures.' 'Georgie Porgie kisses hikers in the woods.' 'Betty Fox like boys . . .' 'Albert goes with Doreen.'

He found the remarks pathetic in their young crudity. He replaced the pile of papers on the table, and as he did so, he was suddenly assailed with feeling of something missing. Something – there was something that ought –

The elusive impression faded as Bland spoke.

'There was no struggle to speak of. Looks as though she just let someone put that cord around her neck without suspecting it was anything but a joke.'

Poirot said:

'That is easily accounted for – *if she knew the person*. In a way, it was what she expected. She was to be the murder victim, you see. She would have let herself be "arranged" for the part by any of the people connected with the Fête.'

'By Lady Stubbs, for instance?'

'Yes.'

Poirot went on: 'Or by Mrs. Oliver, or Mrs.

Legge, or Miss Brewis or Mrs. Masterton. Or for that matter, by Sir George, or Captain Warborough, or Alec Legge, or even Michael Weyman.'

'Yes,' said Bland, 'it's a wide field. Only two people have an absolute alibi, Sir George was on duty at the Shows all afternoon, never left the front lawn, and the same goes for Captain Warborough. Miss Brewis might just have done it. She went between the house and the garden, and she could have been absent for as long as ten minutes without being noticed. Mrs. Legge could have left the Fortune Telling tent, though it is unlikely; there was a fairly steady stream of clients there. Mrs. Oliver and Michael Weyman and Alec Legge were wandering about all over the place – no alibis of any kind. However I suppose you'll insist that we absolve your lady novelist of the crime.'

'One can make no exceptions,' said Poirot. 'Mrs. Oliver, after all, arranged this Murder Hunt. She arranged for the girl to be isolated in the boathouse, far away from the crowds by the house.'

'Good Lord, M. Poirot, do you mean –'

'No, I do not mean. I am trying to get at something which is still very nebulous ... which so far has baffled me. There is another point, the key. When

Mrs. Oliver and I discovered the body, Mrs. Oliver unlocked the door with a key. There was another key which was to be the last "clue". Was that in place?'

Bland nodded.

'Yes. It was in a small Chinese pottery theatre in the hydrangea walk. Nobody had got to that clue yet. There was a third key in the house – drawer in the front hall.'

'Where everyone could get it! And in any case, if someone she knew tapped on the door and asked her to open it, Marlene would have done so. If Mrs. Masterton, say, or Mrs. Folliat –'

'Mrs. Masterton was very much in evidence at the Fête. So was Mrs. Folliat.'

'I noticed that Mrs. Folliat was – how shall I say – playing the hostess.'

'Tis her house by rights,' said Constable Hoskins severely. 'Always been Folliats at Greenshore.'

Poirot stared at him. He missed what Inspector Bland had been saying and only heard the end of his speech.

'– no earthly reason why that girl should have been killed. We'll know better where we are when we've run Lady Stubbs to the ground.'

'If you do,' said Poirot.

Bland laughed confidently.

'Alive or dead – we'll find her all right,' he said. 'Dash it all, a woman can't just disappear into space.'

'I wonder,' said Poirot. 'I very much wonder . . .'

CHAPTER EIGHT

THE WEEKS went by, and it seemed that Inspector Bland's confident statement was proved wrong. A woman *could* disappear into space! Nowhere was there any sign of Lady Stubbs, alive or dead. In her cyclamen clinging Ascot frock and her high heels and her great black shady hat, she had strolled away from the crowded lawn of her house – and no human eye had seen her again. Her frantic husband besieged police headquarters, Scotland Yard was asked for assistance by the Chief Constable, but Hattie Stubbs was not found. In the publicity given to the disappearance of Lady Stubbs the unsolved murder of Marlene Tucker faded into the background. Occasionally there was a paragraph to the effect that the police were anxious to interview or had interviewed someone, but none of the interviews led to anything.

Little by little, the public lost interest in both the murder of Marlene and the disappearance of Lady Stubbs.

It was on an October afternoon, two months after the day of the Fête, that Detective Inspector Bland rang up Hercule Poirot. He explained that he was passing through London, and asked if he could drop in and see M. Poirot.

Poirot replied most cordially.

He replaced the receiver, hesitated, then rang Mrs. Oliver's number.

'But do not,' he hastened to add when he had made his demand to speak to her, 'disturb her if she is at work.'

He remembered how bitterly Mrs. Oliver had once reproached him for interrupting a train of creative thought and how the world, in consequence, had been deprived of an intriguing mystery, centring round an old fashioned long-sleeved woollen vest.

Mrs. Oliver's voice, however, spoke almost immediately.

'It's splendid that you've rung me up,' she said. 'I was just going to give a Talk on "How I write my Books" and now I shall get my secretary to ring up and say I'm unavoidably detained.'

'But, Madame, you must not let me prevent –'

'It's not a case of preventing. I should have made the most awful fool of myself. I mean, what *can* you say about how you write books? I mean, first you've got to think of something and then when you've thought of it, you've got to force yourself to sit and write it. That's all! It would have taken me just three minutes to explain that, and the Talk would have ended – and everybody would have been very fed up. I can't imagine why everybody is so keen for authors to talk about writing – I should have thought it was an author's business to *write*, not talk."

'And yet it is about how you write that I want to ask you now –'

'You can ask, but I probably shan't know the answers. I mean one just writes. Just a minute – I've got a frightfully silly hat on, for the Talk, and I *must* take it off. It scratches my forehead!'

There was a momentary pause and the voice of Mrs. Oliver resumed in a relieved voice.

'Hats are really a symbol nowadays, aren't they? I mean one doesn't wear them for sensible reasons any more – to keep one's head warm, or shield one from the sun, or hide one's face from people one doesn't want to meet – I beg your pardon, M. Poirot, did you say something?'

'It was an ejaculation only. It is extraordinary,' said Poirot and his voice was awed. 'Always – always – you give me ideas . . . So also, did my friend Hastings who I have not seen for many years . . . But no more of all that. Let me ask you instead a question. Do you know an Atom Scientist, Madame?'

'Do I know an Atom Scientist?' said Mrs. Oliver in a surprised voice. 'I don't know. I suppose I *may*. I mean I know some Professors and things – I'm never quite sure what they actually *do*.'

'Yet you made an Atom Scientist one of the suspects at your Murder Hunt?'

'Oh, that. Well, that was just to be up to date. I mean, when I went to buy presents for my nephews last Christmas there was nothing but science fiction and the stratosphere, and supersonic toys! And so

I thought: better have an atom scientist as the chief suspect. After all, if I had wanted a little technical jargon I could have always got it from Alec Legge.'

'Alec Legge? That is the husband of Peggy Legge – is *he* an Atomic scientist?'

'Yes, he is. Not Harwell – Wales somewhere, or Bristol. It's just a holiday cottage they have on the Dart. So of course I do know an Atom Scientist after all.'

'And it was meeting him at Greenshore that probably put the idea of an Atomic Scientist in to your head. But his wife is not Yugoslavian?'

'Oh no! Peggy's as English as English.'

'Then what put the idea of a Yugoslavian wife into your head?'

'I really don't know . . . refugees perhaps . . . or all those foreign girls at the Hostel next door – always trespassing through the woods and speaking broken English.'

'I see – yes, I see . . . I see now a lot of things. There is something else – there was a clue, you said, written on one of the Comics you had provided for Marlene.'

'Yes.'

'Was that clue something like –' he forced his

memory back – '"Johnny goes with Doreen – Georgie Porgie kisses a hiker – Betty is sweet on Tom"?'

'Good gracious, no, no – nothing silly like that. Mine was a perfectly straight clue. *Look in the hikers rucksack!*'

'*Epatant!*' said Poirot – 'Naturally *that* had to be suppressed! Now one more thing. You have said that various changes were suggested in your scenario, some you resisted and some you accepted. *Was it originally your idea to have the body discovered in the boathouse?* Think carefully.'

'No it wasn't,' said Mrs. Oliver. 'I arranged for the Body to be in that little old fashioned summerhouse quite near the house, behind the rhododendrons. But they all said that it would be better to have the last clue far away and isolated, and as I'd just made a great fuss about the Folly Clue, and it didn't seem to me to matter, I gave in.'

'The Folly,' said Poirot softly. 'One comes back always to the Folly. Young Michael Weyman standing there the day I arrived, saying that it should never have been put where it was put . . . Sir George's Folly . . .'

'He had it put there because the trees had blown down. Michael Weyman told us so.'

'He also told us that the foundations were rotten
– I think, Madame, that that is what you felt in that
house – It is the reason you sent for me – It is not
what you could *see* that was rotten – it was that which
was concealed below the surface – You felt it – and
you were right."

'I don't really know what you are talking about,
Monsieur Poirot.'

'Have you ever reflected, Madame, on the enormous part that Hearsay plays in life. "Mr. A said,"
"Mrs. B. told us." "Miss C. explained why –" and so
on. And if the known facts seem to fit with what we
have been told, *then we never question them.* There are
so many things that do not concern us, and so we do
not bother to uncover the actual facts.'

'M. Poirot,' Mrs. Oliver spoke excitedly. 'You
sound like you knew something.'

'I think really I have known it for some time,' said
Poirot dreamily. 'So many small unrelated facts –
but all pointing the same way. Excuse me, Madame,
my front door bell rings. It is Inspector Bland who
arrives to see me.'

He replaced the receiver and went to let his guest in.

CHAPTER NINE

'Two months now,' said Bland, leaning back in his chair and sipping gingerly at the cup of China tea with which Poirot had provided him.

'Two months – and there hasn't been a trace of her. It's not so easy to disappear in this country as all that. Not if we can get on the trail straight away. And we were on the trail. It's no good saying that she went off on that fellow's yacht. She didn't. We searched that boat very carefully, and she wasn't on it – alive *or* dead.'

'What kind of a yacht was it?' asked Poirot.

Bland looked at him suspiciously.

'It wasn't rigged up for smuggling, if that's what

you mean. No fancy hidden partitions or secret cubby holes.'

'That is not what I mean. I only asked what kind if yacht – big or small?'

'Oh it was a terrific affair – must have cost the earth. All very smart and newly painted – and luxury fittings.'

'Exactly,' said Poirot. He sounded pleased.

'What are you getting at, M. Poirot?'

'Paul Lopez is a rich man. That is very significant.'

'Perhaps. But I don't see why. What do you think has happened to Lady Stubbs, M. Poirot?'

'I have no doubt whatever – Lady Stubbs is dead.'

Bland nodded his head slowly.

'Yes, I think so too. We found that hat of hers. Fished it out of the river. It was straw and it floated. As for the body, tide was running out hard that afternoon. It will have been carried out to sea. It will wash up somewhere someday – though it mayn't be easy to identify after all this time. Yes, I'm clear on that. She went into the Dart – but was it suicide or murder?'

'Again, there is no doubt – it was murder,' said Hercule Poirot.

'Who murdered her?'

'Have you no ideas as to that?'

'I've a very good idea, but no evidence. I think she was murdered by Paul Lopez. He came up to Greenshore in a small launch by himself, remember. I think he came ashore by the boathouse and that she slipped down there to meet him. It seems fantastic that he could conk her on the head or stab her and push her body into the water and not be seen doing it – when you consider how many craft there are on the river in the summer – but I suppose the truth is if you're not expecting to see anyone murdered you don't see it! Plenty of horse play and shrieks and people shoving each other off boats, and it's all taken to be holiday fun! The one person who *did* see it happen was Marlene Tucker. She saw it from the window of the boathouse, and so – she had to be killed too.'

He paused and looked enquiringly at Poirot.

'But we've no evidence,' he said. 'And Lopez has gone home. We had nothing to hold him on. We don't even know *why* he killed Hattie Stubbs. There was no monetary gain. She didn't own any property out there and she hadn't any money of her own

– only a settlement that Sir George had made about six months after their marriage. We went into all the finances. Sir George is a very rich man – his wife was practically penniless.'

He gave an exasperated sigh.

'So where's the motive, Monsieur Poirot? What did Lopez stand to gain?'

'Poirot leaned back in his chair, joined the tips of his fingers and spoke in a soft monotone.

'Let us take certain facts in chronological order. Greenshore House is for sale. It is brought by Sir George Stubbs who has recently married a girl from the West Indies; an orphan educated in Paris and chaperoned after the death of her parents by Mrs. Folliat, the widow of a former owner of Greenshore House. Sir George is probably induced to buy the house under the influence of Mrs. Folliat whom he permits to live in the Lodge. According to a very old man formerly in service with the Folliats, there will always be Folliats at Greenshore House.'

'You mean old Merdle? Lived in the cottage down by the quay?'

'Lived? Is he dead?'

'Took a drop too much one night, they think,

coming back from Dartsway opposite; he missed his footing getting out of his boat and was drowned.'

Poirot remarked, 'An accident? I wonder . . .'

'You think it wasn't an accident? Did he know something, perhaps, about his granddaughter's death?'

'His granddaughter?' Poirot sat bolt upright. His eyes shone green with excitement. *Was Marlene Tucker his granddaughter?*

'Yes. His only daughter's child.'

'Of course,' said Poirot. 'Of course . . . I should have guessed that . . .'

Bland moved restively.

'Look here, M. Poirot, I don't understand . . .'

Poirot raised an authoritative hand.

'Let me continue. Sir George brings his young wife to Greenshore. The day before their arrival there had been a terrible gale. Trees down every- where. A month or two later Sir George erected what is sometimes called a Folly – just where a very big oak tree had come out bodily by the roots. It was a very unsuitable place, according to an architect, for such a thing to be put.'

'Daresay George Stubbs didn't know any better.'

'And yet somebody told me that he was a man of quite good taste, surprisingly so . . .'

'M. Poirot, what is all this getting at?'

'I am trying to reconstruct a story – the story as it must be.'

'But look here, M. Poirot – aren't we getting a long way from murder.'

'It is the story of a murder. But we have to begin at the beginning . . .'

CHAPTER TEN

HERCULE POIROT paused a moment at the big wrought iron gates. He looked ahead of him along the curving drive. Golden-brown leaves fluttered down from the trees. Near at hand the grassy bank was covered with little mauve cyclamen.

Poirot sighed. The beauty of Greenshore appealed to him. Then he turned aside and rapped gently on the door of the little white plastered Lodge.

After a few moments' delay he heard footsteps inside, slow hesitant footsteps. The door was opened by Mrs. Folliat. He was not startled this time to see how old and frail she looked.

She said, 'M. Poirot? You?' and drew back.

'May I come in?'

'Of course.'

She led the way and he followed her into a small sitting room. There were some delicate Chelsea figures on the mantelpiece, a couple of chairs covered in exquisite petit point, and a Derby tea service was on the small table. A chosen few of the treasures of the past were here with the old lady who had outlived her kindred.

She offered Poirot tea which he refused. Then she asked in a quiet voice:

'Why have you come?'

'I think you can guess, Madame.'

Her answer was oblique.

'I am very tired,' she said.

'I know. There have now been three deaths, Hattie Stubbs, Marlene Tucker, old Merdle.'

She said sharply:

'Merdle? That was an accident. He fell from the quay. He was very old, half blind, and he'd been drinking in the pub.'

'I do not think it was an accident. Merdle knew too much.'

'What did he know?'

'He recognised a face, or a way of walking, or a manner. I talked to him one day when I was here before. He told me something about the Folliat family – about your father-in-law and your husband, and your sons who were killed in the war. Only they were not *both* killed, were they? Your son Henry went down with his ship, but your second son, James, was not killed. He deserted. He was reported at first, perhaps, *Missing believed killed*, and later you told everyone that he *was* killed. It was nobody's business to disbelieve that statement. Why should they?'

Poirot paused and then went on:

'Do not imagine I have no sympathy for you, Madame. Life has been hard for you, I know. You can have no real illusions about your younger son, but he was still your son, and you loved him. You did all you could to give him a new life. You had the charge of a young girl, a subnormal but very rich girl. Oh yes, she was rich. But you gave out that she was poor, that you had advised her to marry a rich man many years older than herself. Why should anybody disbelieve your story? Again, it was nobody's business. Her parents and near relatives had been killed. She was at a convent in Paris and a firm of

French lawyers acted as instructed by lawyers in San Miguel. On her marriage, she assumed control of her own fortune. She was, as you have told me, docile, affectionate, suggestible. Everything her husband asked her to sign, she signed. Securities were probably changed and re-sold many times, but in the end the desired financial result was reached. Sir George Stubbs, the new personality assumed by your son, was a rich man and his wife was a pauper. It is no legal offence to call yourself "Sir". A title creates confidence – it suggests, if not birth, then certainly riches. And rich Sir George Stubbs, older and changed in appearance and having grown a beard, bought Greenshore House and came to live where he belonged. There was nobody left after the devastation of war who was likely to have recognised him, but old Merdle did. He kept the knowledge to himself, but when he said to me slyly that there would *always be Folliats at Greenshore House*, that was his private joke.

'So all turned out well, or so you thought. Your plan, as I believe, stopped there. You had provided your son with wealth, his ancestral home, and though his wife was subnormal she was a beautiful and docile girl, and you hoped he would be kind to her and that she would be happy.'

Mrs. Folliat said in a low voice:

'That's how I thought it would be – I would look after Hattie and care for her. I never dreamed –'

'You never dreamed – and your son carefully did not tell you, that at the time of the marriage *he was already married*.

'Oh, yes – we have searched the records for what we knew must exist. Your son had married a girl in Trieste, half Italian, half Yogoslavian, and she had no mind to be parted from him, nor for that matter had he any intention of being parted from her. He accepted the marriage with Hattie as a means to wealth, but in his own mind he knew from the beginning what he intended to do.'

'No, no, I do not believe that! I cannot believe it . . . It was that woman – that wicked creature.'

Poirot went on inexorably:

'He meant *murder*. Hattie had no relations, few friends. Immediately on their return to England, he brought her here. And that was when Hattie Stubbs died. On the day of the Fête the real Lady Stubbs had been dead eighteen months – he killed her the actual evening of their arrival here. The servants hardly saw her that first evening, and the woman they saw the next morning *was not Hattie*, but his Italian wife made up as Hattie and behaving roughly much as Hattie behaved. There again it might have ended. The false Hattie would have lived out her life successfully as Lady Stubbs – gradually allowing her mental powers to improve owing to what would vaguely be called "new treatment." The secretary, Miss Brewis, already realised that there was very little wrong with Lady Stubbs' mental processes and that a lot of her half-wittedness was put on.

'But then a totally unforeseen thing happened. A cousin of Hattie's wrote that he was coming to England on a yachting trip, and although that cousin had not seen her for many years, he would not be likely to be deceived by an impostor.

'There might have been several different ways of meeting the situation, though if Paul Lopez remained long in England it would be almost impossible for "Hattie" to avoid meeting him. But another complication occurred. Old Merdle, growing garrulous, used to chatter to his granddaughter. She was probably the only person who listened to him, and even she thought him "batty" and paid very little serious attention when he talked about having seen a woman's body long ago in the wood, and about Mr. James being Sir George Stubbs. She was slightly subnormal herself, but she had perhaps sufficient curiosity to hint at various things to "Sir George". In doing that, she signed her own death warrant. The husband and wife worked out a scheme whereby Marlene should be killed and "Lady Stubbs" disappear in conditions which should throw vague suspicion on Paul Lopez.

'To do this, "Hattie" assumed a second personality, or rather reverted to her own personality. With Sir George's connivance, it was easy to double the parts. She arrived at the Youth Hostel in the role of an Italian girl student, went out alone for a walk – and – became Lady Stubbs. After dinner, Lady Stubbs went to bed early, slipped out and returned to the Hostel, spent the night there, rose early, went out, and was once more Lady Stubbs at the breakfast table! Back to her bedroom with a headache until the afternoon, but, again with Sir George's help, she staged a trespassing act in company with a girl who was also at the Hostel. The changes of costume were not difficult – shorts and a shirt under one of the elaborate dresses Lady Stubbs wore. Heavy white make-up for Hattie, a big Coolie hat that shielded her face; a gay peasant scarf, big spectacles and some bronze-red hair for the Italian girl hiker. I saw them both – and never dreamed they were the same person. It was "Lady Stubbs" who slipped away from the Fête, went to the isolated boathouse and strangled the unsuspecting Marlene. She threw her hat into the river, packed up her Ascot frock and high heeled shoes in a rucksack she had concealed earlier near the boathouse. Then, back to the Fête as the Italian girl, joining up with her casual acquaintance, the Dutch girl, doing a few shows together, then, as she had previously announced to her companion, she leaves by the local bus, an inconspicuous figure. There are forty and fifty visitors each day at the Youth Hostel. They arouse no interest or speculation. Then back to London, to await quietly a suitable time to "meet" Sir George, and eventually to marry him when he can at last presume his wife's death.'

There was a long pause. Then Mrs. Folliat drew herself up in her chair. Her voice had the coldness of ice.

'What a very fantastic story, M. Poirot,' she said.

'I can assure you there has never been more than one Lady Stubbs. Poor Hattie has always been – poor Hattie.'

Poirot rose to his feet and going to the window, opened it.

'Listen, Madame. What do you hear?'

'I am a little deaf. What should I hear?'

'*The blows of a pick axe* . . . They are breaking up the concrete foundation of the Folly. What a good place to bury a body – where a tree has been uprooted and the earth is already disturbed. Then, a little later, to make all safe, concrete over the ground where the body lies, and on the concrete, erect a Folly . . .' He added gently, 'Sir George's Folly . . .'

A long shuddering sigh escaped Mrs. Folliat.

'Such a beautiful place,' said Poirot. 'Only one thing evil . . . The man who owns it . . .'

'I know.' Her words came hoarsely. 'I have always known. Even as a child he frightened me . . . Ruthless . . . Without pity . . . And without conscience . . . But he was my son and I loved him . . . I should have spoken out after Hattie's death . . . But he was my son – how could *I* be the one to give him up? And so, because of my silence – that poor silly child was

145

killed . . . And after her death, old Merdle . . . Where would it have ended?'

'With a murderer it does not end,' said Poirot.

She bowed her head. For a moment or two she stayed so, her hands covering her eyes.

Then Mrs. Folliat of Greenshore, daughter of a long line of soldiers, drew herself erect. She looked straight at Poirot and her voice was formal and remote.

'Thank you, M. Poirot,' she said, 'for coming to tell me yourself of all this. Will you leave me now? There are some things that one has to face quite alone . . .'

THE END

Agatha Christie and the
Greenshore Folly

by John Curran

By the mid-1950s Agatha Christie had reduced her output of books to one title a year, the annual 'Christie for Christmas'. During this decade she consolidated her reputation as a crime dramatist with eight new Christie plays opening in London's West End between 1951 and 1960. This was her golden age of theatre, accounting to some extent for fewer new Christie novels in the bookshops. And it was during this period that a Poirot title with a most remarkable genesis came to be written... and then re-written.

In November 1954 her agent, Edmund Cork of Hughes Massie, wrote to the Diocesan Board of Finance in Exeter explaining that his client would like to see a new stained glass window in the chancel of St Mary the Virgin Church in Churston Ferrers, where

Agatha Christie worshipped. In *An Autobiography* she recalled that 'One thing that gave me particular pleasure was writing a story... the proceeds of which went to put a stained glass window in my local church... I wanted this to be a happy window which children could look at with pleasure'. Ironically, as events were to prove, she describes the story as 'a long-short I think they call it: something between a book and a short story'. The rights to this story were to go to a fund set up for the purpose of installing this proposed window and the author took pleasure in choosing both the artist and the design. The Diocesan Board and the local church were very happy with the arrangement and a letter of 3 December 1954 confirmed 'Mrs Mallowan's [Agatha Christie's] intentions to assign the magazine rights of a long short story to be entitled *The Greenshore Folly*' to such a fund. The amount involved was expected to be in the region of £1,000 (roughly £20,000 in today's value).

By March 1955, however, the Diocesan Board was getting restive and wondering about the progress of the sale. Embarrassingly, for the first time in 35 years, it proved impossible to sell the story. The problem was its length; it was a novella – neither a novel nor a short story – which was a difficult size for a magazine. While this market was a very lucrative one throughout her career, the Queen of Crime frequently had difficulty with its demands. Although they were usually happy to be offered the latest Christie title, editors frequently demanded cuts in the text, normally to accommodate advertisements. As discussed in *Agatha Christie's Secret Notebooks*, the novels *Dumb Witness* (1937), *The Moving Finger* (1943) and *Taken at the Flood* (1948), to take just three examples, all suffered this indignity. And as such serialisations normally preceded book publication it seems likely that the cuts demanded by the editors of their original magazine appearances account for the textual differences between UK and US editions of some Christie titles to this day.

So, by mid-July 1955, the decision was made to withdraw the story from sale, as, to quote Cork, 'Agatha thinks [it] is packed with good material which she can use for her next full length novel'. As a compromise, it was agreed that she would write another short story for the Church, also to be called, for legal reasons, 'The Greenshore Folly', but, as Cork explained, 'it will probably be published under some other title'. So, the original and rejected novella 'The Greenshore Folly' was elaborated into *Dead Man's Folly* and the shorter and similarly titled 'Greenshaw's Folly' was written to swell the coffers of the Church authorities. This replacement story, a Miss Marple investigation, was first published in the UK in *Daily Mail* in December 1956, in the US in *Ellery Queen's Mystery Magazine* in March 1957, and was collected in *The Adventure of the Christmas Pudding* in 1960. Apart from the similarity of title, there is no connection whatever between the two stories and is further proof, if any were needed, of Christie's fertility of imagination.

Perhaps because this was a personal project, written for her place of personal worship, Agatha Christie was anxious to retain a local connection, and it seems clear that from the beginning the story was to be set at Greenway. But it is important to remember that, even on first publication, no one, apart from family and close personal friends, would realise that. Although she had used the grounds of the house before for *Five Little Pigs* (1943), and would use the ferry across the river Dart at the bottom of the garden a few years later in the opening chapter of *Ordeal by*

Innocence (1958), 'The Greenshore Folly' was always intended to feature an extended and detailed use of her beloved Greenway.

With the exception of the entirely fictional folly itself, every location mentioned in both novel and short story exists in reality. The main house, 'a big white Georgian house looking out over the river', is called Greenshore House in the novella, later amended to Nasse House in the novel, but is instantly recognisable as Greenway House, bought by Agatha Christie in 1938. The brief history related by Mrs Folliat is also an accurate, if selective, account of the residence. Both versions of the story also feature the Gate Lodge, 'a small white one-storeyed building… a little back from the drive with a small railed garden round it', Ferry Cottage, the Battery, 'an open space, round in shape with a low battlemented parapet', the Tennis Court, and the Youth Hostel next door. The all-important Boathouse is described as 'a picturesque thatched affair' (it has since been re-roofed), an image belying its use as a murder-site. The internal geography of Greenshore House also reflects Greenway: the drawing-room with its French window, the room across the hall 'lined with bookshelves' with a 'table by the window', and Poirot's bedroom – 'along a passage to a big airy room looking out over the river' – with the bathroom across the corridor. The magnolia tree near the front door where Mrs Folliat and Hattie stand to talk, the drive ending at the big iron gates, the winding and steep path connecting the Battery and the Boathouse – all these exist in reality and can be seen and enjoyed by present-day visitors to Greenway House.

In *Agatha Christie's Secret Notebooks* (2009) I gave an account of the plotting Notebooks of the Queen of Crime; dating from 1915 to 1973, these were where Agatha Christie jotted her ideas, considered her characters, and refined her plots. As she writes in the 'Introduction' to *Passenger to Frankfurt* (1970): 'If one idea in particular seems attractive… [you] work it up, tone it down and gradually get it into shape'. This 'working' and 'toning' took place in the pages of her 73 Notebooks.

Notes relating to *Dead Man's Folly*, eventually published in November 1956, with a prior serialisation in *John Bull* magazine beginning four months earlier, are contained in Notebooks 45 and 47. But as a result of the book's convoluted history, it is impossible to be certain whether the notes refer to the initial novella or final novel version. It seems likely that Notebook 47 is the original 'Greenshore' version and Notebook 45 the *Dead Man's Folly* version. Notebook 47 is a discussion of basic plot points, indicating the earliest toying with ideas. In fifteen pages of this Notebook Christie sketched the entire plot of 'The Greenshore Folly' so when it came to expanding it, she had only to elaborate, as the mechanics of the plot were already established from two years earlier. Although the (possible) title 'The Folly', as well as the more elaborate 'Sanderson's Folly' and 'Grandison's Folly' appear in Notebook 47, a reference to 'Greenshore' would seem to confirm this supposition. Most of the following notes are incorporated into the plot, although the ideas of an accompanying bother and Lady D's lover, as reported by the 'student', are discarded.

Does Sir George marry Hattie Deloran – she is mentally defective – he buys place 'Greenshore' and comes here with his wife – ~~the night~~ a folly has been prepared – she is buried. The Folly goes up the next day

Another Lady Dennison [Stubbs] takes her place – servants see nothing – they go out for a stroll – other girl comes back (from boathouse). Then for a year Sir George and Lady Dennison are well known figures for nine months? For three months? Then the time comes for Lady D to disappear – she goes up and down to London – doubles part with pretending to be a student (a young man really her brother? With her)

She changes her clothes + emerges (from boathouse? Folly? Fortune teller's tent?) as student from hostel – goes back there – has story to tell of Lady D. and lover? Architect?

Further notes outline the opening scene – Poirot's and Mrs Oliver's phone conversation – and other ideas, all of which, with minor changes – garden fete/'Conservation Fete', Girl Guide/Boy Scout victim – were included:

Mrs Oliver summons Poirot – she is at Greenway – professional job – arranging a Treasure Hunt or a Murder Hunt for the Conservation Fete, which is to be held there.

*'Body' to be boy scout in boat house – key of which has
to be found by 'clues' or a real body is buried where tree
uprooted and where Folly is to go*

Some ideas

*Hiker (girl?) from hostel next door – really Lady
Bannerman [Stubbs] wearing long shiny coat + pearls
etc. underneath shorts and shirt*

As she frequently did when plotting a new story,
Christie devised motives and imagined backgrounds
and this listing of 'A. B. C. D.' variations appears
frequently throughout the Notebooks. Of the menu
below, only 'A' is completely discarded; elements
from all three possibilities are included, although
there is no Peter Lestrade in either version.

Who wants to kill who
*A. Wife wants to kill rich P[eter] Lestrade. Has lover
– both poor*
*B. Young wife recognised by someone who knows she is
married already. Blackmail?*
C. P Lestrade – has a first wife who is not dead – (in

S. America?) – it is wife's sister who recognises him
Czech girl at hostel? P mentions meeting a hostel girl
'trespassing' – angry colloquy between them seen (but
not heard) by someone – he decides to kill her
D. Mrs Folliat – a little balmy
or young Folliat at hostel?
. . . .

Mrs Folliat of original family who built it – now
belongs to Sir George Stubbs with beautiful young
wife – Chilean girl? – Italian mother – Creole? – Rich
sugar people – girl is feeble minded. Spread about that
Sir G made his money in Army Contracts… really Sir
G (a pauper) is planning to kill wife and inherit her
money

Alongside her own plot Christie also sketches:

Mrs Olivers plan

The Weapons Revolver
Knife
Clothes line
. . . . .
Footprint (in concrete)

Rose, Gladioli or Bulb Catalogue? Marked?
Shoe
Snapshot

Who?	*Victim*
Why?	*Weapon*
How?	*Motive*
When?	*Time*
Where?	*Place*

This underwent elaboration and refinement and even the two published versions differ slightly. When Mrs Oliver explains her creative process, and its inherent problems, it is difficult not to hear the voice of her creator. And it should be remembered that Agatha Christie devised just such a real-life Treasure/ Murder Hunt many years earlier on the Isle of Man. The resultant story, 'Manx Gold', and the fascinating history behind this unique enterprise, can be found in the posthumous collection *While the Light Lasts* (1997).

A final intriguing note in the preliminary sketch illustrates Christie's by now compulsory exploration of every possible plot variation, despite the fact that on the previous page of the Notebook she had (more or less) decided on the sequence of her story:

Does Maureen [Marlene] *go off for a 'tea break' – girl hiker replaces her? <u>Then</u> girl hiker is murdered.*

This first-ever publication of *The Greenshore Folly* affords readers a glimpse into the creative process of the world's best-selling writer. Unlike other stories expanded from a short story – The 'Market Basing Mystery'/'Murder in the Mews', 'Yellow Iris'/*Sparkling Cyanide* – here the story remains largely the same so it is possible to follow the re-construction . This expansion of novella into novel took place in the pages of Notebook 45 with notes to herself – '*a much elaborated scene*', '*alterations on p.12*', '*detailed questioning*', '*elaborate breakfast party*' – throughout. The 'page 12' reference is, in all likelihood, to the original typescript as she worked her way through it, noting scenes and passages to expand, and appending a timetable clarifying the crucial events:

4.5 pm H[attie] tells Miss B to take tea

*4.10 pm H goes into tent – out of back into hut –
dresses as girl – goes to boat house –*

*4.20 calls to Marlene – strangles her then back +
arrives as herself Italian girl …*

*4.30 leaves with Dutch girl + pack on back?..Dutch
girl goes to Dartmouth – Italian girl to Plymouth*

Finally, and poignantly, note that the lines from
Spenser, quoted by Mrs Folliatt at the close of (iii) of
the novella, and Chapter IV of the novel, are the lines
that appear on Dame Agatha's gravestone in Cholsey
churchyard: '*Sleep after toyle, port after stormie seas,
ease after warre, death after life, doth greatly please…*'

Now, almost forty years after her death, her
legions of fans can enjoy this previously unpublished
example of her art.

Dr John Curran
Dublin
January 2014

AGATHA CHRISTIE (1890–1976) is known through-out the world as *The Queen of Crime*. Her first book, *The Mysterious Affair at Styles*, was written during the First World War and introduced us to Hercule Poirot, the Belgian detective with the 'Little Grey Cells', who was destined to reappear in nearly 100 different novels or short stories over the next 50 years. Agatha also created the elderly crime-solver, Miss Marple, as well as more than 2,000 colourful characters across her 80 crime books.

Agatha Christie's books have sold over one billion copies in the English language and another billion in more than 100 languages, making her the best-selling novelist in history. Her stories have transcended the printed page, also finding success as adaptations for stage, films, television, radio, audiobooks, comic strips and interactive games, and her many stage plays have enjoyed critical acclaim – the most famous, *The Mousetrap*, opened in 1952 and is the longest-running play in history. Agatha Christie was made a Dame in 1971.